I0788790

broken love story

NATASHA MADISON

Cover Design: Melissa Gill with MGBookCovers & Designs

Book formatting: CP Smith

Editing done by Jenny Sims Editing for Indies

Proofing Julie Deaton Author Services by Julie Denton

Dedication

Michael, may you find someone who loves all of you.

Chapter One

Blake

"Twenty minutes, guys," I say, flipping the flapjacks that I'm making. I'm on my fourth shift of six at the firehouse station, and my duty this week is cooking. I fucking hate it, especially the lunch duty.

However, since we got a call early, we missed breakfast, so I'm doing the easiest thing. Half the guys sit at the wooden table drinking coffee while the other half either lounge on the couch or sit outside in the nice sunny weather.

"Did you guys hear that Squad 47 got a DOA?" asks Ricky, the firehouse chief, coming into the room.

"Tough," one of the guys says. "Never a good fucking day when you have a DOA," Colin says, turning the page to the newspaper he's reading. I nod my head in agreement.

I look at Wyatt. "Is the bacon almost done?" I ask him. "This is the last flapjack."

"Be done in a second," he says, pushing away from the splattering grease of the bacon. I place the flapjacks on the counter next to the eggs that Simon scrambled. Wyatt turns and places the sausage and bread next to the eggs, then turns to grab the bacon.

"Ring it," he says, talking about the bell we always ring when a meal is ready. Going over, I press the little doorbell button. The line has already formed by the time I turn around a couple of seconds later. By the time everyone is sitting down, almost nothing is left. We are a group of eight firemen and four paramedic techs.

"One more twenty-four-hour shift and I get to sleep in my own bed," Colin says, and we all nod.

The food is eaten and the plates are piled in the sink for the clean-up crew, which is my second least liked job in the house. As I step out of the kitchen, my phone rings, showing me that my cousin, Crystal, who is an emergency room nurse, is calling.

"Hey," I answer.

"There was an accident." I'm expecting her chipper and happy voice, but instead, she speaks monotone, and I know, I feel it in my fuckin' gut, that something is wrong. I hold my breath, waiting for it, but nothing, fucking nothing could prepare me for the name she throws out. "Eric." My sister Hailey's husband. My legs almost give out as I hold the wall, Colin and Wyatt both looking at me. My hand covers the phone. "My brother-in-law," I say as they both look at me with their mouths open for two seconds, then nod that they have this. I grab my keys off my locker shelf, running out of the building.

"Where is he?" I ask right away. Getting into my truck, I screech my tires as I peel out.

"He was DOA," she finally says, the defeat in her voice apparent. "There was nothing." My emergency training pops up, and I start issuing orders.

"Call Hailey and tell her I'm on my way. I'm four minutes out." I hang up the phone and then call my parents.

My father answers on the second ring. "Hello?"

"Dad, it's me. I need you to get Mom and meet me at the emergency room," I say, zigzagging in and out of traffic to get to my sister's house.

"Bad?" It's the only question he asks.

"Yes," I tell him. "It's Eric," I finally say, my voice cracking.

"I'll leave now." He hangs up, and I call Colin next.

"Brother," he answers right away.

"The DOA this morning," I say as I turn on Hailey's street, "was Eric."

"Fuck," he hisses out. "I got you covered. We already called Logan, and he's on his way."

"Thank you," I say, disconnecting as I pull up to Hailey's house.

I don't know how much Crystal has told Hailey, so I get out, jog to the front step, and open the door. I spot my sister on the phone as she turns around to face me. Her life is about to change, and she might not ever be the same person again. A piece of her is gone, a piece that might never mend.

I look in her eyes and see the tears already forming. I hold my hand out to her, and the hand holding the phone slowly lowers to her side. She looks at me in confusion, not sure what is going on, and I don't know if I have the answers for her. I do what I need to do—I give her as much of my strength as she needs. I follow her out of the house and help her in the truck after she opens the door.

Her eyes look at me, asking me a million things, but I know my eyes don't give anything away. It's the training—never let them see your sorrow, never let them see you broken. I've had ten years of practice and not just at the academy. I buckle her in, and the only thing I can muster up to say is, "It's going to be okay."

She nods her head, then I step back and shut the door, jogging over to my side. As I drive, I look over at her watching a bird fly above, her eyes following its every movement.

She watches the bird so intently she doesn't even realize I've stopped the truck and I'm opening her door. Her eyes look at me, glazed over, almost as if she isn't there. Almost as if her body is closing herself off from the sadness and horror she is about to witness. "You're going to be okay," I assure her as I raise my baseball cap to run my hands through my hair.

"What's going on?" She finally finds the words to ask. The question pleading for me to tell her it's all a mistake, but I don't answer. I grab her hand and walk inside the revolving door to the emergency room. We walk silently down the corridor, her hand squeezing mine now. She looks up at me, asking one more question. "Is it Mom? Dad?" I can't answer her; my heart beating for her can't give in to the answer. I'm afraid I won't be strong enough for her. I'm afraid that my grief from ten years ago is going to surface, and she doesn't need that right now.

Her eyes go back to the floor, and her question is answered when my parents step forward. My mother has tears running down her cheeks, and my father has his arm around her shoulders. They are standing next to the nurses' station. She looks back at me in horror. "Is it Nanny?"

I don't answer because Crystal comes out from behind the nurses' station in her everyday uniform of blue scrubs and Crocs, wearing a stethoscope around her neck.

Hailey takes one glance at her face, and her feet stop in their tracks. I look back at her, trying to lead her to them, but she doesn't move; nothing moves except her knees when they start to give out and the most horrendous cry of pain comes out of her. I don't get to her in time before her knees hit the floor and she's on all fours. The look she gives all of us lets us know she knows; she knows that somewhere in this busy hospital emergency room, her husband lies dead.

Crystal rushes to her as she holds her in her arms, the tears soaking into her blue scrubs. I bend to pick her up, my body cocooning hers. I carry her to the white fucking room no family ever wants to step foot into. The room where the walls are stark white and not one picture hangs on them. Where four chairs line one side with a single chair facing it. The room where you go, and in five seconds or less, they tell you that your loved one who you prayed for, who you tried to make promises for is gone. That nothing you could have done or said would have changed the outcome.

Crystal gets up, and I go to her, pulling her to my side. "What the fuck happened?"

"It was a head-on collision," she says in a low voice, hoping that no one really hears us. "He was DOA." I close my eyes, the pounding forming behind my eyes is almost too much to bear.

"Where is he?" Hailey's soft voice finally says. My father turns to her, trying to tell her something, but she snaps, "I need to see him." I know from her tone that it isn't a request, it's a demand. She needs to see him with her own eyes; she needs to see that this isn't just a dream. She needs to sit by his side and hold his cold hand for her to know he isn't coming back. She needs to sit there beside his body that will slowly start changing color while she asks the only question she can ask, "Why?" I look down at my feet as the memories from ten years ago try to enter my mind, but I block them. This isn't the time. I look up and hear Crystal try to tell her that whatever picture she has of Eric, she doesn't want one of him lying on that bed.

I look past her and see two officers approaching. Frank and Landon come in, and I see it right away, the brown fucking bag. I groan inwardly as I think about the fireman on the scene who collected the things and handed it to them. The last of whatever remains of the victim. I don't have to listen to the speech that Frank gives because it's almost the same speech we tell the fire victim's family who waits on the scene. "I'm sorry for your loss." What a crock of shit. I lean against the wall, putting my head back. I need a fucking drink.

I see Hailey just nodding, but her eyes never leave that brown fucking bag. Crystal drags her away from everyone and walks into another room. Frank comes over to me, extending his hand. "I'm …" I grab his hand, holding my other one up to stop him from the speech.

"I know," I say, and he nods at me. We all know.

"If there is anything that you guys need, let us know," he says, and that is the way it is—firemen, cops; it's all family.

I don't have a chance to say anything because Crystal yells my name, and I rush into the room where they disappeared.

I pick Hailey up, waiting for someone to say something, but I know she's in shock. She has to be in shock. This morning, she got up with her husband, probably sat at the table as they made plans for the night or even the weekend, and now she goes back home alone. The plans a distant memory.

"She is in shock. What do you want to do?" Dr. Arnold says. "We can keep her here, or you can take her home."

"Home," Crystal and I both say. "The last thing she needs is to be in a room two feet from her dead husband," she whispers to me. I turn around, picking Hailey up and carrying her back to my truck. I drive her home; this time, the drive is even more dreadful than before.

I look over at her as she clutches that brown fucking bag so tight her fingertips are white. There is no vise that will pry that bag out of her hands.

Chapter Two

Blake

We pull up to Hailey's house before I even have a chance to make a plan. I jump out of the truck, open the passenger door, and unbuckle her, then help her get out.

Crystal follows us as we walk up the step to her house, their house. Eric and Hailey's house.

I walk in and take in the house. You know right away Eric is home. He was an engineer for aircrafts and was always on the road. But when he was home, you knew right away because his things would be all over the house. A tossed sweater here, an empty mug by the couch. And now is no different. His sweater is tossed over the couch. Hailey walks over to the mug left beside the couch and picks it up.

"He just got home last night," she whispers at us, looking up. "Maybe if he didn't come back, he would still be here. Maybe …" She trails off in a whisper. Crystal looks at me, telling me silently to get rid of anything that shouldn't be out of place. I know what she means by just a look and walk to the kitchen to place his mug in the sink. His laundry is draped over one of the chairs.

Crystal takes her upstairs while I try to take things down that will remind her of Eric, but I know it's all for nothing; nothing will make her forget. I'm leaning against the counter with my head hanging down when the front door opens and my mother and father walk in.

"Where is she?" my mother asks Crystal, who has just walked back down the stairs. Her jacket is tossed over the couch, right next to Eric's sweater.

"She is sleeping or resting," Crystal answers her quietly. "I don't even know anymore." I watch her walk into the kitchen and go to the cabinet that holds the whiskey. She comes to the counter, reaching for a glass, and takes a couple of shots. My mother walks into the kitchen, placing the brown fucking bag on the counter.

"You want one?" she asks me, and I just nod my head. I don't want just one shot; I want the fucking bottle. She pours three fingers into the glass, and I pick it up and swallow it in one shot, feeling the burning all the way down.

"How the fuck did this happen?" Crystal asks the question everyone is wondering. *How in the fuck did this happen to us again?* "I'm going to go up and lie with her in case she wakes up in a panic."

I nod my head as she walks out of the room. "There is so much that needs to be done," my father says from the kitchen table as I pour another shot. "Arrangements that need to be …"

He stops talking, or I stop listening. I think it's a mixture of both when I pour myself another drink; this time, it goes down even smoother than before. "I think I'm going to go for a drive," I say to them, and they nod. "I'll be back in an hour."

I grab my keys, start the truck, and pull away from the house. While I'm driving, my mind swirls all over the place as I pass the black-iron gate, turning left and then taking the second right.

I stop as the sun starts to go down, the sky almost pink. I walk through the grass, making my way to the small little tombstone.

Francesca Marie Bianchi

Beloved Daughter and Sister

June 5, 1980 – July 5, 1999

"Hey, Frankie," I say. Sitting in front of her tombstone, I feel a peace settle in me. "How you doing today?"

When I first set eyes on Frankie on the first day of high school, my heart stopped. Her long brown hair flowed in the wind. Honest to God, it was like that moment in The Wonder Years *when he meets Winnie. I just knew, knew in my heart, she was the one. I was fifteen when we had homeroom together, and I thought that it was definitely a sign. Then we were on the same debate team, and what started as us being study partners turned into so much more.*

Loving Frankie came so easy; she was just carefree about everything—nothing fazed her, nothing upset her, it just was. Her motto was "Even if you get angry or mad, it won't change anything."

I shake my head. Until she turned eighteen, when she started feeling sick. It just wouldn't go away; nothing she did made her feel better. One day, I took matters into my own hands and got her dressed to take her to the doctor, but I didn't have to leave her house because she sat me down.

"I know why I'm sick," she said, avoiding my eyes.

"Did you go to the doctor already?" I asked her, finally relieved that she was going to get better. She had lost so much weight.

"I did about two weeks ago." She finally looked up, and her brown eyes were filled with tears.

"Well, you should have gotten better already, so we need to go back." I started to get up, ready to take her to the hospital.

"Blake, I'm not going to get better," she whispered as one lone tear rolled down her cheek. A cheek I'd held in my hand, a cheek I'd kissed, a cheek that hid a secret dimple that only came out when she was really, really smiling. "I have leukemia."

Three words cut me off; three words that took away my world. That night, I went home and researched everything there was to know, but nothing, nothing, prepared me for what was to come.

We did everything the doctor said, everything down to the T, but in the end, the disease won, and she was nothing but a shell of the vibrant woman I once knew. I begged and pleaded with her to fight. I begged and pleaded with God to spare her. But no one listened; her parents didn't think I would stick around, but an army of Navy SEALs couldn't keep me from sitting by her bedside. Nothing could stop me from begging her to be my wife; nothing could stop me from loving her so much that when she took her last breath, I died as well. Breathing was hard to do because the pain in my chest never went away. Fuck, it still lingers. My hopes, my dreams—everything got buried the day we lowered her casket into the ground. I went through the motions, pretending I was okay when inside, I was empty. I was hollow; it was gone. My heart was still beating, my breath was still coming, but I wasn't there.

My hands trace the letters on the tombstone. "Miss you, baby," I say. When I feel a soft breeze go by, it's almost as if she answered me today. "So much," I say, the tears coming no matter how much I fight them. No matter how much time goes by, the tears always come. I stay here for twenty minutes, lying down in front of her plaque with my head resting on my arm. Leaning forward, I kiss her name. "See you next week," I tell her, getting up and walking back to the truck. Making my way back to my sister's house, I hope someone is going to be able to give her the strength she needs to go on.

The drive back to Hailey's house is quiet as night falls. The stars are coming out; some are blinking, some just lighting the sky. My mother and father are in the kitchen, and my mother is cooking.

"You think she's going to eat any of that?" I ask them. Heading for the bottle of whiskey still on the counter, I pour one shot after another. The numbness never comes, so I sit down and look at my father, who shoots his eyebrows up at me in question. "Don't."

"We have to eat and keep up our strength for your sister," my mother says.

I hear squeaking on the stairs and know that's either Crystal or my sister. "She's up," Crystal says. Walking into the kitchen, she grabs the bottle of empty whiskey. "You couldn't even save me a shot?" I don't answer but look up at her. We both look at the hallway when more creaking sounds. Hailey comes into the kitchen with her hair tied on top of her head, wearing Eric's robe. Her eyes are swollen from the tears she has shed all day.

"Hey." Crystal walks to her, whispering, "You hungry?" Hailey looks around the room at the table that my parents set, then spots the brown paper bag on the counter. She turns on her feet, going straight to the brown bag. My eyes find Crystal, and we both take a big inhale.

The sound of the crinkling bag fills the silence of the room as the four of us stand, waiting for her to fall. Waiting to catch her.

Opening the bag, she takes out his watch first, and looking at it causes the sobs to rip out of her. She brings the watch to her nose to smell it, her other hand gripping the counter for support. I step forward but stop when she sets it down. I don't see what she brings out next because the tears block my vision.

"This isn't his." She turns to us, showing us a black iPhone. "His phone was white."

Crystal walks over to her, this time to help her stand. "Maybe it was put in there by mistake. Here, let me plug it in, and we can see who the phone belongs to." She grabs it from her and walks over to the wall charger, plugging it in.

Hailey finally finds his phone. Running her fingers over it, she closes her eyes as tears drip off her chin, almost as if you left the faucets running. "We took this picture last week after he got home. He was gone for a month this time. It was the longest he was ever away." She looks up at us, the hollowness almost too much to bear. "How did this happen?" She looks at each of us separately as she waits for an answer. My mom and I are brushing our own tears off our face when the buzzing on the counter starts.

Hailey walks over to the phone and picks it up. Her face goes white, whiter than it was, her lips almost turning an ash. Her hands start shaking, shaking so much the phone slips out of her hand and lands right in front of her feet, the screen shattering. Little did we know that shatter would change the path of everyone's life.

Chapter Three
Samantha

"Let's go, guys, or we are going to miss the bus!" I yell up the stairs toward my girls, Liz, who is eight, and Daisy, who is five.

"The bus is going to be here in two minutes!" I yell again, walking back to the kitchen and picking up my now cold cup of coffee.

I pick up my phone to check for any missed calls or messages, and the only thing that greets me is the picture we took two months ago. Our four happy smiling faces when Eric and I had just found out we were expecting baby number three.

While I sat on the toilet in our bathroom, a whole mix of emotions coursed through me. I always wanted a big family. Doesn't everyone who is born in the system wish for everything they didn't have?

I never had a mother; I never had a father. I never had siblings; I never got into a fight with my sister because she borrowed my clothes and didn't tell me or vice versa. My parents were out there somewhere, or maybe they weren't. I had no idea.

My mother was a crack addict. I know that for sure because I was born a crack baby, which is the reason I didn't get adopted right away. No one wanted the burden of the extra care; no one wanted to be the parents to "that baby."

So although I grew up and the crack left my system, I was never adopted.

Foster parents weren't willing to take me either. Nope, I was the lucky one who was always in the group home for unwanted kids. I kept my head down, and my mind on the prize. The prize that when I turned eighteen, I would leave that roach-infested home and be able to create my own perfect life.

The day I turned sixteen, I got a job at the local diner. I busted my fucking ass to work and maintain a GPA of three point five. When college came around, I knew that if I didn't qualify for assistance, I would never be able to attend. With rent and all that, I knew I couldn't do it. That was the first time in my life I regretted ever being born. Although my GPA was high enough to be accepted, the fact that I had no money coming in meant that the loan was denied. So after sobbing into my pillow for a straight six hours while I asked God why he hated me so much, I got my journal out and made a plan. I would graduate; it would just take me a long fucking time. I would take two courses a semester, and eventually, I would graduate and become a social worker.

Strange, I know, but I wanted to be "the social worker" to make miracles happen, especially for girls and boys like me who got left behind. Kids were not just a case number but actual people.

My first apartment had more roaches than the foster home. Fuck, I remember sleeping with a hat on just so they wouldn't crawl into my ears. But the first of my luck changed when a new co-worker started. She had just moved into town and was looking for a roommate. Same rent as what I paid now, but the utilities were going to be shared, so I jumped on it. My life was just starting to pan out when I walked to a table late Saturday night, early Sunday morning.

"What can I get you?" I asked the blond boy sitting there opening five or six books.

He didn't look up. "Coffee, just lots and lots of coffee." When he finally looked up, my stomach went into a loop. He had the clearest blue eyes I'd ever seen. "Just keep it coming." He smiled at me, and his dimple made my heart sputter. Nodding at him while I looked down at my notepad, I was hoping to God I wasn't blushing.

I looked back up at him, smiling shyly. "Coming right up." I turned and walked away and watched him for the next seven hours as he studied. He came back the next night, and the night after that. His smile made my belly flip and my heart race, and when he finally got the nerve to ask me out, I couldn't say no.

"Has Daddy called?" Lizzie's question snaps me out of my daydream.

I shake my head. "Not yet," I say sadly, the whole time actually fucking cursing him. Lately, he's just fucking absent, and I hate it. "Maybe when you get back." I smile at her as Daisy runs down the steps one at a time, picking up her backpack.

"Let's go to the bus." I kiss Lizzie's head, grabbing both girls' hands, and walk them to the corner to wait for the yellow school bus. "Have a great day at school," I tell them when the bus pulls up, and they climb on.

I make my way to my house, our house—another dream come true for me. Walking inside, I go to the kitchen to clean up the plates from this morning. Once everything is finished, I pick up my phone to call Eric.

"Hey, you've reached Eric, leave a message."

I breathe out. "It's me. The girls tried calling you last night and this morning. I know you're busy, but can you call me back?"

I toss my phone down, making myself another cup of coffee.

My stomach turned and roiled, my hand resting on my now empty stomach. Our third baby was not meant to be. Two days after we found out, I miscarried. I didn't know what to think about it. If I'm honest, it was a relief to both of us.

The pregnancy was a shock, especially with Eric's crazy travel schedule.

He's hardly home anymore, and when he's here, he isn't really here. I had a mini breakdown seven or eight months ago because I thought he was cheating. I looked for the signs, even looked in his phone when he was sleeping, but didn't find anything. Even when I sat him down as I cried in his arms, he told me I was being silly and crazy. But something was there, something I couldn't explain or put my finger on. I'm lost in my head today, so much so I don't even notice the leak coming from the dishwasher till it's all over my floor.

"Fuck," I say, running to get towels to mop it up. It takes me a full hour to finally get the floor clean. I pick up my phone and call my brother-in-law Elliot, who answers on the first ring.

"If it isn't my favorite sister-in-law," he says, laughing.

I roll my eyes. "I'm your only sister-in-law." I laugh. Eric has two brothers, Elliot, and then his younger brother, Ethan. If there wasn't a difference in ages, you would think they were triplets.

"Okay, you got me there." He laughs. "But no matter what, you'll always be my favorite."

I shake my head, smiling. "Because I cook for you and wash your clothes." With Eric out so much, Elliot usually joins us for dinner whenever he can, but lately, it hasn't been that much. I think he has a new girl, and it's getting serious. "My dishwasher is leaking again."

"Where is Eric?" he asks.

"He left yesterday," I answer and then look at the clock. It's almost pickup time. "Do you think you can come and look at it?" I ask him. "I'm making chicken enchiladas."

He groans. "Fine, twist my arm. I'll be there after I finish work," he says, and I hear a drill in the background. He's a mechanic who just opened his own shop in town.

"Thank you," I say, hanging up the phone and walking out the door to the bus stop. The kids bounce off the bus, and I bend to kiss them both.

"How was school?" I ask them, and Lizzie tells me about the solar system project she needs to have done for tomorrow that she forgot about. I groan inwardly because I hated the solar system. "We can YouTube and Google and see what we come up with." I grab her by the shoulders, bringing her to me; she is getting so big.

The first thing the girls do is unload their lunch bags, throwing all the things in the garbage or the sink. I walk over to the computer with Lizzie, and we make a plan for the solar system. "We need to run out and get supplies," I tell her as I call for Daisy, who comes hopping into the room. "We need to go to Michael's for Lizzie's project," I tell her, and we all load up the minivan. We spend the next fucking three hours cutting Styrofoam balls and painting them different colors.

Daisy has a meltdown because I won't let her use the glue gun, and then again when I won't let her paint. I'm at my wit's end when she calls out for Daddy with her last breakdown.

I pick up the phone to call him, going into another room. His voicemail picks up again. "Seriously, this is fucking ridiculous," I say, angry with the fact I'm having to do a solar system project, angry that my five-year-old is having a nervous breakdown because she's tired, angry that for the past fucking eighteen months, he hasn't really fucking been here, and I've fucking had it.

The hormones in my body are still fucking all over the place, my body doesn't know if I'm having a baby or not, and it's just the straw that broke the camel's back. I hang up right when Elliot walks in and looks at me.

"You okay?" he asks, coming to me.

"No, I'm not okay. Your brother isn't answering, Lizzie forgot about a project that she needs to do, Daisy is overtired and just crying about everything. I've kind of just reached my limit." He doesn't say anything, just goes into the kitchen.

"I heard someone needs some help," he says, and Daisy finally gets up from the floor, running to him. "Daisy girl, why the tears?"

"Mommy didn't let me glue and cut." She wipes the tears from her cheeks with her palms. "Or paint."

"Well, it's dangerous." I let him explain to Daisy what I just tried to explain to her for the past two hours. Going to the stove, I take his plate out of the oven. He looks up, smiling when he sits on the chair. Picking Daisy up on his lap, he eats with one hand. I finish the project with Lizzie while Elliot gets his tools out and asks Daisy to be his helper.

That lasts a whole five minutes before I hear crying from the kitchen and then Daisy runs in. "I want Daddy," she says, and I murmur, "You aren't the only one."

I pick up my phone again to call his number, and this time, it connects after two rings. Fucking finally.

"Hello?" a shaky female voice answers his phone, and my stomach drops. The back of my neck gets hot, and my heart starts to pound so loud, it feels like it's coming out of my eardrums. My hands shake and get sweaty.

"Hello," I answer, my voice almost as shaky as the woman who answered. "Who is this?" I ask her now, my voice coming out a little bit higher as I wait for her to tell me who she is. I think I know, I think my heart knows, but in the end, I knew nothing. Because the next few words cut me to my core. It is like he stood over me with a knife and stabbed me right in the heart. "This is Hailey."

"Who is Hailey?" I ask, waiting for the dreaded answer. Waiting for the confirmation of what I know deep inside.

"Who are you?" she asks me, not willing to tell me who she is.

"I'm his wife," I say, and the shattering of her phone fills the silence. Just like that, my world falls apart, and my knees now give out as I fall to the floor.

They say that when something happens to you and your body goes into shock, you remember key things from that day. I will never smell lemon again without thinking of the day my life changed. I will never listen to a certain song without being transported back.

Your brain shuts off and goes into itself as it takes in certain little things, like the heat on your face as you drive down the street and the sound of chirping birds in the distance as they soar in front of you. The constant beat of your heart in your chest as the sound echoes in your ears like galloping horses. This is how you survive, I'm told. This is how my story goes. This is how my perfect life became broken.

Chapter Four

Samantha

"Hello?" Another strange voice comes on the phone as my head starts to turn and my eyes start to see white spots.

"Who is this?" I now ask in a whisper again.

"This is Crystal." she says. "Who is this?"

"Samantha." My voice cracks as a sob tries to come out, but I push it down. "Who are you guys, and why do you have Eric's phone?" I look around to see if I can get Elliot's attention, but I'm alone. I'm sitting in my living room with a picture of the two of us hanging in the middle of the room. My two girls beside me as I sit here and find out where my husband is.

"Are you …" Crystal stops and then asks, "Who are you to Eric?"

"I'm his wife," I finally say. The sadness leaves me, replaced with anger. "And I'm about tired of answering questions without getting any of my own."

"I …" She stops, and then I hear her breathe out. "Where are you?"

"I'm at home," I answer her right away.

"I need you to sit down." It's there again, the pain; the pain that turned to anger comes back. I look at Lizzie, who looks at me with tears running down her face, and Daisy, who has curled up beside me and is looking up at me, hoping I have the answers. "There has been an accident."

"Oh my God," I whisper, and the sob that I was holding back now comes ripping through me. The shrieking and pain, running up my throat so hard, fast and loud, my throat burns.

"Is he okay?" I ask between the sobs.

A man's voice comes on. "He didn't make it." Four words that take whatever is left of me.

"Mommy," Lizzie says beside me. "Mommy, are you okay?" The tears stream down my cheeks, my chest starts to go up and down, and my breathing is so hard. My free hand goes to my chest, hoping to get the pain to go away.

"Where"—I try to catch my breath, try to calm myself down before I pass out—"where is he?"

"He's at Mercy General Hospital." His voice goes soft. "I'm sorry for your loss, but I have to know who are you?"

"I'm his wife," I say again. How many fucking times do I have to tell these people that I'm his wife? "We've been married twelve years. We have girls." My voice fades off when I hear shouting.

"What the fuck is going on?" Elliot finally says, grabbing the phone out of my hands. With everything going on, I didn't even see him walk in. I didn't notice him standing over me; I didn't notice anything. "Who the fuck is this?"

"Where is Samantha?" the man asks right away.

"She's right next to me. Now, answer my fucking question," he says. I don't know what the other guy says, but Elliot's eyes close, and his head falls back as one tear escapes him.

"Fuck," he hisses. "Where is he? Who is this?" My knees give out, and I fall to my butt, sitting down. My girls crawl on my lap, and I hold them both, rocking from side to side while humming their favorite song that I used to rock them to bed with. My eyes close as I try to focus on the fact that I'm all alone, by myself. He's gone. The man who took me out of the shitty life I was handed and gave me everything I ever dreamed of on a silver platter.

He gave me love, he gave me protection, and he gave me two brothers, but most importantly, he made me a mother. I block out the words; I block out the angry tone of Elliot's voice. I block it all out.

"That's impossible," he now whispers. "He's already married."

He hangs up and slowly peels Daisy from me, carrying her upstairs. I hear his voice in a whisper as he walks downstairs. "I just called Ethan, and he's on his way." He grabs Lizzie, who had fallen asleep silently sobbing in my lap.

I'm still sitting in the middle of my living room when he comes back downstairs. "What just happened?" I want him to tell me it's a dream, to tell me that it's not true.

"I have no fucking idea, but by the end of tonight, I hope we all know the answers."

"Who were those people?" I ask him right when the front door opens, and my in-laws, Judy and Adrian, enter. My mother-in-law sits down next to me, taking me in her arms.

"Oh, honey," she says while she strokes my hair, and I cry in her arms. Another thing he gave me was a mother and a father. Someone who welcomed me with open arms, with love and support. "It's going to be okay."

I don't say anything as we both cry—me for my husband, her for her son. When Ethan arrives, he sees us sitting in the middle of the living room. My father-in-law stands with Elliot, and they talk in whispers. "I came as fast as I could."

"You need to go with your brother," Adrian says to him. "Go to this woman's house and grab his stuff." His voice comes out bitter and angry. "I already called the lawyer."

"What?" I ask, looking up at him. "What lawyer?"

"It's not for you to worry about now," he says with his lips pressed together. "You have enough on your plate."

"I need to know," I tell them, my mother-in-law's hands falling from me.

Elliot grabs the back of his neck with his hand and starts talking. "She needs to know." He looks at his father, who glares at him. "Apparently, he was married to this woman named Hailey."

I gasp out in shock, my hand going to my mouth. "What?"

The thought of him having an affair is beyond anything I could understand, but marrying this woman? This faceless woman, how could he?

"They got married six months ago," Elliot whispers and then stops when his father cuts in.

"Doesn't mean shit. He gave them the wrong name," he hisses. "You are to go there, get his body and all his belongings, and come back." He puts his hands in his pockets. "Papers are being drawn up as we speak."

"What papers?" My throat is dry.

"Nothing to concern yourself about," he says, turning to Ethan. I look at Elliot, and he just shakes his head. "Go before it gets too late. I have Phillip meeting you at the hospital to bring his body home."

Oh my God, the words are too much as the sob comes out, and I cover my mouth with my hand. Elliot comes over to me and picks me up, his hands around my shoulder as he carries me upstairs and places me in the bed. "Listen to me," he says as my body shakes with sobs. "I have to leave, but I will tell you whatever you need to know when I come back." I nod my head, tucking my knees to my chest as I watch him walk out of the room. I watch the doorway for the next five hours, flipping the pillow over four times from the tears that have soaked it.

The pain of him being gone, the pain of him not explaining to me what just happened, the pain that my daughters will never get to grow up with him. He will never walk them down the aisle; he will never have their first dance together. He is just gone.

When I finally hear the front door open, I sit up and walk to the staircase. My head's spinning, so I sit on the steps, listening.

"I need a drink." I hear Elliot say, opening the cupboard and taking out what I'm assuming is the scotch we kept in there.

"Who wants one?" he asks, and I hear Ethan grunt.

"So did you meet her?" my mother-in-law asks.

"Oh, yeah," Ethan says. "We sure did," he hisses.

"Bitch," Judy says. "What kind of a woman takes another man's wife?"

"Well," Elliot now talks, "he lied to her, so I don't really think it's all her fault." I walk down to the kitchen quietly as I listen to them talk. "He used his middle name and told them he was an orphan."

"He had to have had a reason," Adrian says, and I close my eyes. "Whatever the reason, I don't give a shit. We are to never talk about that woman or her family. She is never to be discussed. No one, and I mean fucking no one, can know about this."

"What are you talking about?" Ethan asks. "Dad, he married this woman, and they had a house together. He had another fucking family. How do you sweep that under the rug?" He doesn't ask any more questions as Adrian's hand hits the table.

"Not a fucking word. For all we know, that woman is insane and lying through her teeth. The lawyer has drawn up the papers, and she is going to be served today."

I walk into the kitchen now, catching the four of them sitting at my kitchen table off guard. The solar system project neatly put away. The four of them look over at me. "Served what?" I look at them, one at a time, but Ethan and Elliot are the only ones who look down. "What?"

"We are serving her a cease and desist," my father-in-law says, "and a restraining order against you and the kids."

"What?" I whisper, my hand going to my chest. "What for?"

"We don't know anything about this woman. We don't know if she is crazy or if she will come after you and the girls," he says, and Judy nods.

"We have to protect you and the girls." Judy gets up and walks over to me, wrapping me in her arms.

"Don't worry about this. Let him take care of it. Let us take care of you." She hugs me in her arms as I sob out again. I let her walk me back upstairs to my bed and lie back down, thinking they are just looking out for me and the girls. They are just looking out for our safety and well-being.

This is what families do, right? They protect you, they shelter you from the pain, and they help you when you're down and can't stand. I have no one to ask; I have no one to tell me the difference. Little did I know … little did I know.

Chapter Five
Samantha

Standing in front of the full-length mirror in my room, I smooth down my black skirt. My blond hair is tied up in a ponytail, my cheeks are sunken in more than normal, and the blackness around my eyes indicates I haven't slept well since this whole thing happened. Since I found out that not only did my husband die, but that he also married someone else.

I sit on the made bed and look down at my wedding band. My thumb of my right hand touches it, and the lone tear that falls out of my eye lands straight on it. "Mommy." I look back at Lizzie, who is standing in the doorway wearing a black one-piece dress similar to mine with ballerina flats.

My mother-in-law went shopping yesterday and bought us all new outfits for today. "We need to put our best foot forward," she said as I watched her walk in with the six bags. "We can't let people talk."

I turned around and walked out of the room, going upstairs. Shutting myself in my bathroom with my back against the door, I cried quietly, trying to hide my sobs. "We can't let people talk," I whispered to myself. The hatred I had begun feeling when I remembered my husband.

Lizzie walks to the side of my bed and sits next to me. "I hate this dress," she says when I put my hand around her shoulder and bring her to me, kissing her head.

"I know, baby," I whisper, "but after today, it's going to be all over."

"That's what Grandpa A said." She mentions the name she calls my father-in-law. Grandpa A because you can't get better than an A.

"Is everyone ready?" I hear Ethan yell from downstairs. "The limo is picking us up in twenty."

"Let's go, baby," I tell her, getting up and holding her hand while we walk downstairs. My in-laws are both sitting in the kitchen. My mother-in-law in a black skirt and top while my father-in-law has on a black suit. "Where is Daisy?" I ask them.

"Elliot is upstairs changing her. She spilled milk on her dress," Judy tells me, looking at Lizzie. "You look like such a big girl." She blinks her tears away.

Elliot comes down the stairs with Daisy on his hip, smiling at me when he walks in. "Okay, you girls go sit in the living room while us grown-ups talk," my father-in-law says, and the girls both know to leave the room. When he knows they are both out of earshot, he starts. "Today is going to be tough, tough for us all, but we have to stand together. We have to be the family that we are." I lean against the counter while he talks. "The situation with the other one has been taken care of, and she has been served papers." I look at him and then at Elliot and Ethan, both of them looking down when our eyes meet. It's almost as if they feel guilty for meeting this woman. My father-in-law continues, "After all this is done today, we are meeting with the lawyers in person, so we can go over the will, start the paperwork for the insurance, and make sure she doesn't touch a thing that belongs to him." I stop listening at this point, turning to look out the window at the backyard.

The swing set that he built in one day to make sure the kids could use it when he left the next day. The patio set he had delivered to us, so I could have somewhere to sit while I watched the girls while he was living with another woman. I shake my head, walking out of the room. I sit on the couch, and the girls come to sit next to me, one on each side. "Today is going to be really hard," I whisper to them, "but we have to be strong for Daddy." They both look at me, their eyes exactly like their father's. "But, if at any time, you need to leave or you need me… I don't care who is talking to me or who is around; you come and get me."

"Grandpa A said we had to sit and wait," Daisy whispers just as Elliot comes into the room and kneels in front of us.

"What is this meeting about?" he asks, smiling at us. The circles around his eyes are just as black as ours. He hasn't left our house since this happened.

"Mommy said if we need her that we can go to her," Daisy says, looking at him and then me, "even if Grandpa A said no."

He leans in, whispering, "You can come to me too, and I'll make sure that you get Mommy."

"Okay," Lizzie and Daisy both whisper at the same time, and then the doorbell rings.

We get up, put our jackets on, and one by one file into the black limo that has come to take us to the funeral home. We arrive before everyone else. "We get an hour with him, and then they will open the door," Adrian says as Judy grabs her tissue and dabs her eyes.

I look around the funeral home. I'm not sure what I'm looking for, not sure where he is. I haven't seen him since he kissed me goodbye four days earlier. His last words to me were, "Call you when I can." That phone call never came.

I follow my in-laws to the big brown door that is closed. "I want to go in before the girls." Everyone turns to look at me.

"We can keep them in the lobby," says the lady who greeted us at the door. She told me her name, but I just didn't listen.

I nod at her as she turns to ask the girls if they want hot chocolate. Daisy's eyes get big as Lizzie turns to look at me. I nod my head, giving her permission, so she can go with the woman.

The doors open, and I don't even know what to expect. I've never been to a funeral. Never known anyone well enough to pay my last respects. Judy and Adrian walk in first, followed by Ethan, and Elliot waits with me. I step foot into the room, and it's so cold that I shiver. The smell of flowers hits me right away, making me turn my head. The number of flowers and wreaths shocks me; the whole room is almost full. Some wreaths blocking others. Rows and rows of brown chairs line the room, all facing toward the front of the room. My eyes land on the brown wooden casket at the front of the room. The open half showing you the white satin inside. I walk down the aisle toward him, and then my eyes land on him. Eric. I can't take another step forward because my knees give out, and I fall. Elliot isn't fast enough to hold me up, and my knee lands with a thud. But the pain doesn't matter because nothing could take the place of the pain in my heart. The sound of wailing fills the room as I look up at my dead husband.

I feel arms around me; I feel myself lifted; I feel myself almost floating. He isn't the Eric who kissed me goodbye; he isn't the Eric who I made promises to; he isn't the Eric who made all my dreams come true. This isn't him.

The man with makeup caked on his face isn't my Eric. My sobs overtake my body as I look at him, expecting him to open his eyes. Expecting something, anything but this. "I want the casket closed," I say, my voice soft. "I want it closed."

"Samantha," my father-in-law starts, "it's—"

I shake my head. "I don't want the kids to see him like that," I say softly. I know that for me they wouldn't even consider it, but for the girls, they would move heaven and earth. "They need to remember him alive and smiling, not like that," I say, pointing at the casket.

"Dad," Ethan says after me, "I agree."

"Me too," Elliot says from beside me. "Close it."

He just nods at us, then walks to the man standing in the corner. The man looks at him as they have a hushed conversation and then just nods his head. "Do you need some water?" Ethan says to me, and I nod. I don't bother listening to what else he says; instead, I get up and go to the casket. Standing before the brown box, I look at him, *really* look at him. You see some bruising under the makeup, and his nose is a little swollen. His hands are folded over his stomach, resting on his black suit. The suit he wore when we got married. *Why?* I ask him in my own head. *Why did you do it?* I ask him, hoping I can hear him whisper something to me, whisper anything back. To answer my questions, to give me something; anything to make me understand why he did what he did. Why he left me with so many fucking questions and not one answer.

The man comes over to close the casket. Eric's face disappears slowly, the shadow filling his face till the casket finally shuts. "I'm sorry for your loss," the man says, nodding at me. "If at any time you want it open, we can open it back up." I turn around now, looking at the chairs that will fill up as soon as the people start coming in. Ethan consoles my mother-in-law, and Elliot stands where we were just sitting, his hands in his pockets.

"I'm getting the girls," I tell them and then walk out with my head held high but my shoulders slumped. Defeated is a word that you use so many times not really understanding what can actually defeat you. I know now, my husband dying, him cheating on me, my kids without a father, my dreams of growing old with him gone. Beaten straight down to my core, straight down to my bones.

I walk over to them as they look up. "Let's go, girls," I tell them as they both get up and walk to me. Lizzie takes one hand, Daisy takes the other, and we walk back into the room that holds a piece of our hearts. The room where their father lies, with no answers and no tomorrow.

We stand in that room for four hours while people come up to me and give me their condolences. I nod my head and play the part of the grieving wife. I am the grieving wife, but I'm also the wife whose husband didn't love her enough to just be with her. The wife who knew her husband was slipping away but couldn't catch it in time. The wife he said he would love and protect. The wife who stands here between his girls wishing that for one second he suffered horribly. The wife who has to pick up the fucking pieces and lie to her girls about what a great guy he was. The wife who, at the end of the day, just wasn't good enough.

We listen as people tell us how amazing he was, how much he loved his family, and how much he loved his girls. The whole time, I'm yelling on the inside, ready to stand in the middle of the room, throw my head back, and yell at the top of my lungs. But I don't do what I want. I don't tell them what a fraud my husband was. I don't tell them that it was almost all lies. I don't tell them that the day he died, they called his other wife and not me. I don't tell them that I wasn't the one with him when he died.

I stand here thinking about this other person—his other wife—and wonder how she would handle this. How she would be with my in-laws. Would she just let them control her and do everything for her? Would she want it to be open and weep for him beside the casket instead of standing next to it?

I look around the room at all the people who came to pay their respects, and my eyes find someone I've never met before. Someone I've never seen before, and our eyes connect. His green eyes stare into mine as I watch him nod to me and turn to walk out. As he walks out of the crowded room, I strain my neck to watch his back. I don't have long to think because Elliot comes up and whispers, "It's time."

Chapter Six

Blake

I walk out of the funeral home with my head down. I make sure not to make eye contact with anyone in case I actually know them. Coming here today was something I know I shouldn't have done, but I did it anyway.

Three days ago, I had to sit my sister down on the couch and tell her that her husband really wasn't her husband. That he had another family. I had to do the dirty work of a coward. I had to take the brunt of her hatred when his two brothers showed up on her doorstep to claim his body. I had to be there while she slowly died right in front of me. And then if that wasn't enough, the fucking cease and desist letter along with the restraining order were served. I wanted to get into my car that minute and find his family, but the last thing my family needed was for me to end up behind bars. So I stood in the corner and developed a plan.

Then I left quietly in the middle of the night, just as the sun was rising, and made my way toward the place where my brother-in-law would be.

I walked into the room, looking around. My eyes landed on the woman I assumed was his wife. I took in her blond ponytail and no makeup on her face. Her brown eyes, red and puffy from the tears that she kept wiping away. Two beautiful little girls stood beside her, and I was okay till she looked my way. When her eyes settled on mine, I saw the anguish she was going through, I saw the pain of losing her husband, and I saw the pain of having to be there, but I also saw something else, something I didn't expect to see. After watching long enough, I saw the anger, and as more and more people approached her, the more her eyes changed from sadness to all-out anger. I looked in her eyes for one second and then left. I couldn't take it; I couldn't breathe. The tie around my neck got tighter and tighter. I pushed out through the door, loosening the tie, then unbuttoned the first button. I opened my door and got in, finally breathing normally for the first time since I walked into that room. The video montage of Eric played on the wall with all the memories from when he was born till he died. Nothing, not one thing would make you think he was a lying piece of shit. Not one mention of the other woman he left behind. Nothing about the woman who has to be carried up to her bed every single night, the one who cries in her sleep, and the one who wakes up every single day with one question on her lips—*why?*

I sat here in the car, not realizing that the people were now walking out of the funeral home. As the hearse pulled up in front of the home, and the casket was carried out by his brothers, who I believe was his father, and three other men. Samantha and his two girls walked out hand in hand with a woman next to them. The two girls looked ahead—the older one with tears in her eyes, and the younger one, leaning on her mother looking like she needed a nap.

They placed the body in the hearse, and the family got into the limo, waiting for them. I watched them pull out of the parking lot, the limo following the casket. I waited till I was one of the last cars left in the parking lot before I finally pulled out and made my way home.

For the next three weeks, I watch my sister fall deeper and deeper into an abyss. I watch her die a little bit more, and I'm powerless to help her. I'm finally off shift from the fire station when my phone rings.

"Hey there." I hear Crystal's voice low and almost in a whisper.

"Hey, yourself," I breathe out. "What's up?"

"I'm going to see her," she says as I hear a car door close.

"Going to see who?" I ask, not sure who she is talking about.

"The wife," she says. "I have to go see her."

"I don't think that is such a great idea. Honestly, what good can come of that?" I ask her, thinking about how she can possibly answer this.

"I have to know what she's like. I have to know for Hailey," she says, and I know that I have to take her. I don't think she will be able to hold back. I pick her up and then follow the address she gives me, pulling up to the quiet little house.

"You sure about this?" I ask Crystal when I finally turn off the car. She looks around, not saying anything but nodding her head.

It's been three weeks since Eric has died, two weeks since his brothers came to the house and 'claimed' all his belongings. Two weeks since Hailey was served with papers demanding she cease and desist using Eric's name.

I get out of the car, looking at the little gray house with flowers lining the walkway. The brown door with the hanging welcome sign. Crystal looks down at her feet, takes a deep breath, and then starts to walk toward the house with me following right behind. When we get to the door, Crystal reaches out to ring the doorbell, and we hear the sound from the open window upstairs.

We hear footsteps approaching the door. "Here we go," Crystal says, and I hold my breath as the door creaks open.

The door swings open, and there standing in the middle is the woman who has haunted my dreams since the funeral. The woman who in my dream is lost and turns to me for help, but each time I'm about to reach out to her and help her, she vanishes right through my fingertips. The woman with blond hair that is straight and long, coming over her thin shoulder. Her big brown eyes, too big for her face, her cheeks more sunken in than before. Her clothes look like they are five sizes too big for her. "Can I help you?" Her voice comes out soft as she looks from Crystal to me. Her eyes stop on me, but she doesn't say anything more.

"I'm Crystal." Samantha's eyes go big when she recognizes the name.

"We are sorry to just barge in on you," I start saying when she looks at me again. It's the same look she gave me at the funeral, except now there is more, there's so much more, and I can't put my finger on it. "We were wondering ..."

Samantha moves out of the way. "Please come in," she says as we walk in. "Don't take off your shoes," she says to us as she turns and walks into her house. The entrance is closed in, and when we walk into the home, we both stop in our tracks. Pictures of Eric are all over the walls; pictures of his family fill the whole wall in the living room. Pictures of him and the girls littered the room.

Samantha turns around and watches us look at all her pictures. "That was taken the day we found out we were expecting our third child. Two weeks later, I miscarried." She points at the big portrait of the four of them. "Would you like to sit here or in the kitchen?"

"I can't sit in this room," Crystal says, but at that moment as I'm looking at Eric in the picture, I know that if he was still alive,

I wouldn't be able to stop myself from destroying him. "It's just too much." Samantha nods her head as if she understands.

"Would you like something to drink?" she asks, going into the kitchen.

"Water," Crystal says. Samantha goes to the fridge, opening the door, and we see the drawings on the fridge. "I can't fucking ..." she mumbles as I place my head down and count to ten. I count to ten and curse him all the way to hell.

She comes back, handing us each a bottle. "I don't know what the protocol is for any of this, so I don't want to be rude in any way." She crosses her hands over her chest, and there it is, the anger that was in her eyes.

"We just want to talk," I finally say. She nods at me and walks to the table.

"I need to sit down." She almost collapses in the chair. Crystal sits in front of her, and I take a seat beside her.

"Are you okay?" I can't help but ask her. I love my cousin, but if this is going to push Samantha over the edge, we aren't doing this fucking closure shit.

"No, actually, I'm not okay. I'm the opposite of okay," she sighs. "I have to pick the girls up in an hour," she starts and then puts her hands on the table as she wrings her fingers. My hands itch to reach over and squeeze them, to tell her it's fine, it's going to be okay, but I don't know that.

"Did you know?" Crystal asks the one question everyone has been dying to ask; the question that could have changed everything.

Her head shakes from right to left. "Not a fucking clue." She wipes a tear from her face. "How long were they together?" she asks, and it's so fucking clear that we aren't the only ones looking for answers. We aren't the only ones questioning everything.

"They were married for the past six months and dated for

about eighteen." Crystal tells her the truth. It's not about lying; it's about fucking closure—for her and for us.

She nods her head. "I just thought we were going through a rough patch." She doesn't try to wipe away the tears this time. "I even felt him get distant, and we spoke about it." She sniffles as we listen to her. "He said it was all in my head."

"Do the kids know?" I have to ask. I have to know, but she shakes her head.

"My in-laws will not permit me to tell them anything except that he died in a car crash." Her voice comes out in a whisper, and I have so many more questions to ask, but I don't. I sit here the whole time watching her, looking at her, studying her.

"Your in-laws are not your boss!" Crystal shouts, and I see something flicker in Samantha's eyes. A war is raging, but I'm not sure for what. And then she cuts me off at my knees.

"I'm a foster child. I grew up in the system. They are the only family I have, so they are not the boss of me, but they are my family." She now sits up. "It is also none of your business how I handle *my* children." Bull's-eye. Don't fuck with Mamma Bear.

I feel Crystal beside me about to freak out, so I place my hand on her arm as she says, "You're right; they aren't my business. You aren't my business, but my cousin, his other wife, is my business." I'm afraid it's too late because her voice continues to rise. "You had your fucking closure; you got to say goodbye to him. She didn't." She glares at her, but Crystal is too far gone. "She had to sit in the middle of their fucking living room and read a fucking cease and desist letter, telling her that everything they had meant nothing. That is my fucking business."

"You done?" Samantha asks, and Crystal nods her head. "You think I had closure because I got to see him in a box? He was dead. You think just because I got his body that I got closure? You think it was easy for me to be the obedient wife and mourn by his casket when all I wanted was to tell everyone what a fucking fake he was. If you think I got the better end of the deal, that is where you're wrong." She stands up now. "Your cousin gets to have the time to cry and ask questions while I have to hide my pain and all my tears because I have two girls who I have to live for. I have to cry into my pillow at night so they don't get up and ask me, "Do you miss Daddy, Mommy?" when the whole time I don't fucking miss him, I fucking loathe him. He made a mockery out of our wedding vows. He made me look like a fucking fool. Do I have his name, yeah, but I would give it back to him. The only thing I can't hate him for is giving me my girls." She swallows. "When I look in their eyes, that are just like their father's, I can't hate him. So don't sit there and think you know anything, when you know nothing."

"We are very sorry," I say to her, and she puts her hand up to stop me as she turns and looks at me.

"Please spare me the fake sorrow. I don't have the privilege to bash him and his ways because my in-laws hold him on a fucking shrine. I can't look at them and tell them what a piece of trash their son was because then I will be left by myself. I play the wife role, and I take the well wishes of the people who come up to me, but at night, when all the lights are off and the kids are tucked into their bed, I'm left picking apart every single memory I have"—she raises her voice—"and it's a lot more than eighteen months."

"This was a mistake." Crystal looks at me, and I couldn't agree with her more. Coming here was a mistake; me going to the funeral was a bigger mistake.

"You came here to see who I was, and I get it. I wanted to do the same. I wanted to meet the woman who he felt he loved so much that he lied and married her. But I can't because at the end of the day those girls need me." I get up, nodding to her, as Crystal walks out of the house without another fucking word. I walk down the step to the car, buckle my seat belt, and look straight ahead as I drive away from the gray house.

"Well, that was a good idea," I finally say when we are far enough away. "Great fucking plan that was."

"She is more broken than Hailey is," Crystal whispers. "Hailey can forget about him, but she will never be able to move on."

"You going to tell her about this?" I ask her, and she nods. "When?"

"When she can handle it. Right now, the only thing she can handle is her bottle of wine. It's got to fucking end."

I agree with her. "Give her another week." I don't turn to look at her.

"Another week." She throws her hands up. "I don't give a shit what you say or that you're older than I am and wiser. Next week, the tough fucking love starts."

"Deal"—I look over at her—"and I won't even give you a hard time about how you treated Samantha." She rolls her eyes. "She isn't the enemy."

She doesn't bother to answer me; instead, she looks out the window, lost in her own thoughts, leaving me to get lost in mine.

Chapter Seven
Samantha

I listen for the front door to close, and then close my eyes until I hear the sound of two truck doors shut. Only when I hear the truck drive off do I open my eyes and look down at my trembling hands. I get up and walk to the sink, turning on the water and filling a glass. I drink a couple of sips and then count to ten. My hands never stop shaking. I look out at the swing set in the backyard and see one of the swings moving slowly with the breeze. The images of Eric looking back at me while he built it. The girls running around him the whole time. The glass in my hand falls to the sink, shattering.

"I hate you." I look around the kitchen, seeing his picture on the fridge along with the kids' drawings. I pull it off the fridge and trace his face with my finger. "I fucking hate you," I whisper to him, hoping that he hears me. Hoping that somewhere, wherever he is, he knows how much I hate him.

The front door opens, and I hear Judy. "Hello!" she shouts, walking into the kitchen. "Oh, good, you're here." I look up at her. "I thought we could have dinner here tonight." I nod my head, putting the picture back on the fridge. It's been three weeks, and in that time, my in-laws have never left my side. Neither have Ethan or Elliot.

"That sounds like a plan." I smile at her, the smile forced this time as Crystal's words linger in my mind. "I have to get the girls soon. Do you need me to help you cook?" I know right away the answer to that is no; my mother-in-law is hands down one of the best cooks and people I know.

"You go sit and rest." She smiles at me as she sets down the bags. "Relax. I have this covered." I just nod at her, then walk upstairs to my bedroom. Looking around, I see little touches of Eric. His shirt still hangs on the chair where he left it; the change from his pocket on his bedside table. I walk to the chair and pick up the shirt, smelling it. His scent still lingers a bit. Did he ever wear this shirt with her? Did he ever hug her in this shirt? Did he tell her he loved her while wearing this shirt that the kids and I bought him for his birthday? Did she unbutton it and slip it off his shoulders?

I take the shirt, wrap it in a ball around my hand, and then throw it in the trash. One down, a million more memories to erase. I turn to walk back downstairs. "Is everyone coming over tonight?" I ask as my mother-in-law looks up from cutting the chicken.

"Yes, I told them to be here at six," she says as I nod my head.

"Good," I say to her as I run through the conversation that will happen tonight. "I'll go get the kids," I tell her, walking out and making my way to the bus stop. Sitting on the sidewalk, I bring my knees to my chest and rest my head on them. He never picked the kids up at the bus stop, even when he was home. I get up when I see the yellow school bus coming down the road, and I smile when I see Daisy hop down the last step. "Hello, lovebug." I bend to kiss her, then stand, looking for Lizzie, who comes down the step wearing a sad little smile. "Hey there." I smile.

"Hey." She turns, heading to the house.

"Is everything okay?" I ask her, holding Daisy's hand.

"Yeah, Mom," she says. I know something is wrong, but I just let it go. We all grieve in different ways, and the only one who really doesn't understand is Daisy, who just this morning wanted to know when Daddy would be home to put her star decals on her ceiling.

"Grandma is at our house cooking," I tell them as we walk ever so slowly home. "How about we have a girls' weekend on Saturday and Sunday?" I ask them, and they both look up at me. "What do you say? Pizza, nail painting, Disney movies, and Chinese food with only us girls?"

They both smile, and I see my Lizzie's eyes light up. "So Friday, as soon as the bus drops you off, it's on." They are all smiles when we walk into the house, and Judy is there to greet us.

"There are my grandbabies." She holds out her arms so they can give her a hug. Lizzie gives her a side hug, quickly patting her shoulder, while Daisy puts

her small arms around her waist.

"We are having a girls' night on Friday," she tells her. "So you and Grandpa can't come."

"But I'm a girl," my mother-in-law jokes with her, "so I can, but Grandpa can't."

Daisy shakes her head. "Nope, just the three girls," she says, walking around her to put her lunch bag on the counter.

"Please start your homework," I tell her as she grabs her green plastic binder and brings it to me. "Let's see what you have." I open it, checking the things that she needs to do while I get her situated. I look over and see that Lizzie has retreated to her room. I make a note to check on her later when it's just us.

For the next three hours, they do their homework, I prepare

lunches for the next day, and my mother-in-law finally finishes dinner. Lizzie and I set the table, each of us helping the other. "Thank you, baby girl." I kiss her head while she wraps her hands around my waist.

Adrian, Ethan, and Elliot all walk in at the same time. Elliot goes right upstairs to take a shower while the other two grab a beer and sit on the couch in the family room to watch the news. When Elliot comes back down fifteen minutes later, he kisses the girls hello, squeezes my shoulder, and then goes to kiss his mother hello.

We sit down at the table, holding hands all around as we say grace. The conversation is about everyone's day. I pick at the food on my plate more than I eat. Looking over at Lizzie, I see she is doing the same thing. "Eat," I tell her, and she just shrugs her shoulder.

"I'm not very hungry," she says, not looking up. Instead, she's scooting things around on her plate to make it look like she's eaten, but I know for a fact she's only taken two bites.

"Are you sick?" Judy asks, putting a hand to her forehead. "She isn't warm."

"I'm just not hungry, Grandma," she says, then asks to be excused.

"I have homework to do," she says, taking her plate to the sink. I watch her walk upstairs, then look at Elliot who just nods at me.

"I'm finished too," Daisy says, slipping out of her chair and carrying her plate to the sink. "Can I go play?" she asks, and I just nod.

"So," Adrian starts, "the lawyer called me today and let me know the will is ready to be read. Sammie, we need to go see him on Friday," he says, and I look up at him.

"Why didn't he call me?" I ask, surprised.

"I didn't want you bothered with any of this. You have enough to worry about with the kids." He smiles at me.

"I know that you guys are trying to help," I say, putting my fork down and pushing the plate away from me, "but we need to go back to our normal."

I look around the table, seeing Ethan look down and then up. "Ethan, you used to come for dinner once a week max."

"But, I-" he tries to say, but I put my hand up.

"It's fine." I smile at him. "It's more than fine."

"And you"—I point at Elliot—"you sleep here tonight, but tomorrow, go back to your apartment."

"You kicking me out of the house?" Elliot smirks at me.

"Yes," I say. "Plus, I think your girlfriend is one step away from leaving you."

"Fuck her," my father-in-law says, and my head snaps back in shock. "Family comes before everything."

"Yeah, Dad," Elliot says as I tilt my head, looking at him as he looks down at his hands.

"No," I say a little louder. "Everyone needs to start living their own lives, and we need to start living our new one."

"If Eric was here," my mother-in-law starts to say, but Adrian puts a hand on hers.

"If he was here, we would have dinner with you guys on Sunday like we did every single week," I start saying, "but he isn't here. He's gone."

"Sam," Ethan starts, "we just want to be here for you and the girls."

"And I love you guys for it, but"—I swallow—"what if he didn't want you guys here?" The tear rolls down my cheek so fast I can't stop it. "What if I wasn't the one he wanted you guys to console?"

Adrian smacks the table, some of the forks clattering on the plates. "You are the one he was married to," he starts, "and that is all that matters. That other woman is a disgrace to her family by living with a married man."

I bite my lower lip. "She didn't know," I whisper. "From what they told me, she had no idea."

"And who told you this?" he asks, his eyes going small as he glares at me.

"Well, her cousin did." I don't bring up Blake. I don't bring up that they sat at this exact table this afternoon as we shared stories.

"Bunch of fucking liars," he says, pushing away from the table. "They better stay where the fuck they are, and if that bitch thinks she is going to get a cent of his life insurance policy, then she is so mistaken. I stopped her once, and I'll do it again."

"You stopped her?" I ask, confused by what he just said.

"She tried to claim his life insurance policy a week after he died."

"What policy?" I ask, looking around the table. None of the three make eye contact with me. "Tell me. You guys obviously know, so ..."

Elliot starts first. "Sam, my father took care of it. What difference does it make?"

I push back from the table, my heart beating a mile a minute. "It makes a huge fucking difference. Tell me." I cross my arms over my chest.

Ethan looks at Elliot, who looks at his father, who finally says something. "They had a life insurance policy together, and the money-hungry woman tried to cash it in. Luckily, we had the lawyer prepared for it, and they blocked her. They also froze their joint account. The money should be in your account as soon as we have everything squared away."

"Joint account?" I whisper, but Adrian continues.

"Lucky for that woman, the house was in her name, or else I would have put it into foreclosure, and she could have ended up in the middle of the street."

"He loved her," I tell them, and he looks at me. "Why are we blaming her?"

"If it wasn't for her, Eric would have never ..." Judy starts.

"Oh, please," I say, rolling my eyes. "He is the only one to blame for this," I finally say, and it feels good!

"Don't say that," Judy says with a tear rolling down her cheek. "H-he just had a lapse in judgment."

I laugh now. "Yes, well, marrying another woman, and living with her while he pretended he was an orphan is definitely a lapse in judgment."

"Sam," Ethan says quietly.

"Maybe if you were a proper wife, he wouldn't have gone out looking for more," Adrian says, and my head snaps back as if he just slapped me in the face. The gasp of shock from everyone around the table stops him from talking.

My heart starts to pound as my neck gets hot. I look down at my hands and then look up, the tears not stopping as they fall onto the table. "I guess you're right on that; if I was half the woman, maybe, just maybe, he wouldn't have wanted anyone else," I say, turning to walk out of the room. I expect one of them to call out to me. I expect Judy to come and hold me and tell me he's just being a jerk. I expect Elliot to tell his father to shut up and that was uncalled for. I expect that and so much more from a family who cares and loves me just like their own, but what I get is nothing. I get no one rushing after me. I get no one coming to hold me as I cry in the middle of my bed. I get no one knocking on the door. I. Get. Nothing.

The knock on the door never comes, but what does come is Lizzie. She lies down in front of me on the bed, her eyes taking me in. "It's okay, Mom," she tells me as she rubs my face. "We have each other."

My hand cups Lizzie's face as I look at my little girl who grew up overnight. "That is all we need," I whisper to her. I listen for the voices downstairs. I listen to the door open and close. I listen to the plates being washed and put away. I listen to Elliot telling Daisy that it's bath time. I listen to all that while I look out the window and Lizzie falls asleep in front of me. She cried so silently beside me I didn't even notice, but her tears wet the pillowcase.

I finally get up when I see that the house is now dark. Walking into Daisy's room, I find her fast asleep. When I turn to walk out, Elliot stands in the doorway of the spare room where he sleeps. "Sam," he says quietly, but I just walk past him. "Will you—"

I turn around to face him. "I get it," I start. "I get that, with this whole thing, the only thing you and your family care about are the girls. And Eric."

"It's not that." He shakes his head, crossing his arms over his chest.

"Do you know that I waited for one of you to come after me? I waited, holding my breath, for one of you to come and tell me that he was wrong. That no matter what I did, it wouldn't have changed what Eric did because Eric was the one who made the mistake. But I sat there on my bed, crying, and the only one who came to me was Lizzie. The only family I have, who I love, who I count as my own, never even came or fought for me."

"Sam." He takes a step forward, and I step back.

"It's fine." I turn. "In the end, I guess the only family I truly have are my girls."

I don't bother listening to him talk. I close the door, silently, quietly, hoping not to wake Lizzie. I lie down and watch her, silently vowing never to let her down.

Chapter Eight
Samantha

"Come on, girls!" I yell up the stairs at them. It's been two days since our dinner with my in-laws. One day since Elliot came over, and twelve hours since he last sent me a text checking on me. It's also been two days since I've spoken to any of them.

My heart is just broken; not only did I lose a husband, but I feel like I lost my family also. I shake my head, blinking away the tears. Not fucking today. "It's girls' weekend, so the faster you get on the bus, the faster the day is over," I say with a smile.

Lizzie comes down first, then Daisy. "I want red on my nails," she says, skipping to get her bag. "Or purple."

Lizzie and I both laugh at her. I walk them to the bus and then go back home to my morning routine. The phone rings at noon, and when I pick it up, I see it's Judy.

"Hello," I say softly, my heart pounding. It feels like I just got into a fight with my best friend, and she is calling me afterward. I don't know how to act.

"Hey," she says just as softly. "Adrian just wanted to remind you about the lawyer. You need to be there at two. I can get the kids from the bus if you are running late."

"Okay, I'll text you if I'm running late," I tell her, and I wait. We both wait. The silence lingers; I'm waiting to hear her say that he was wrong. I'm waiting for her to say anything, but she doesn't.

"Okay. Let me know," she says as she disconnects. I look down at the phone. She didn't even ask how I was doing or how the kids were doing. Nothing. I sit on the chair in the kitchen looking at my phone, waiting for it to ring again. I'm waiting for her to call me back and say sorry I didn't ask how you were doing, to ask about the kids, to ask if I'm okay, to ask if I need anything. Anything. Instead, I get nothing.

I put my phone down and look out the window, lost in my thoughts, lost in my memories. The tears just stream down my face when I think that for the last twelve years, this family has taken me in with open arms and tears while I walked down the altar to Eric.

Stood by me when I walked across that stage to accept my diploma, cheering the loudest.

Watched me pregnant with two babies, rubbing my belly as they leaned in and spoke to the girls in the hopes to feel the baby kicking. Judy held my hand when I miscarried and cried, telling me everything happens for a reason. She held me when Eric died, and I tripped over his shoe. Now, now it's like she doesn't know me. My chest hurts, the pain ripping through me, the pain almost unbearable as I place my head on the table and sob. This time, no one is here to hold me; this time, no one is here telling me it's going to be okay. There is no one.

Peeling myself out of the chair, I walk upstairs and step in the shower, but no amount of cover up can cover the blackness under my eyes or their puffiness. I slide into my black jeans that had fit me tight at one point but now are a little baggy. I pair it with a white V-neck sweater and grab my black jacket off the hanger. I slide into my black heels and throw my hair in a bun on the top of my head.

Grabbing my purse, I make my way over to the lawyer's office. Stepping in, I smile at the receptionist and give her my name.

"Mr. Feldman is ready for you." She escorts me down the plush beige carpeted hallway to the corner office.

Knocking, she gestures for me to enter. The man sitting behind the desk rises to his feet and walks around the desk, his salt and pepper hair matching his mustache.

"Nice to meet you, Mrs. Schneider." He extends his hand, and I shake it, just nodding at him. "Please have a seat." He points at the two chairs facing his desk. I look at the family pictures on the bookshelf behind his desk—the one of him and his wife, the one of him with his children, the one with him and who look like his grandchildren. My eyes go back to his as he puts on his glasses. "I'm so sorry about your loss. Eric was a great man." I'm almost tempted to roll my eyes or pfft out. Please fucking spare me; if he was such a great man, then why the fuck did he feel the need to live a double life? Why?

I have a box full of questions, but the only one that keeps repeating is why? Why the fuck would you do it? Why would you? And then it was always how could you do this to me? To the girls?

"So," he starts, "Eric's will is pretty standard. Everything is left to you, of course." He turns the papers, explaining his stocks and everything that I am inheriting. "He did have in here that his father is the one in charge of the money to be issued out on behalf of the girls."

I look at him. "I don't understand?" I ask him.

"It means that the girls' money is in a trust, and the executor is Mr. Schneider. So if you would want something for them, it would have to be approved by him.”

“I’m sorry, that is wrong because we both had the same will.” I think back to when we signed the will. We were both in charge of everything if the other one left. “If you can check mine, you will see that it isn’t like this.”

“He amended his copy six months ago,” he says, and my heart beats so hard and fast, I’m pretty sure that he can hear it. The sound must be filling the silence of the room as he looks at me. “It’s really just a precaution to make sure the girls’ needs are met, and that the money is allocated.”

“Unbelievable,” I say under my breath. “Is there anything in there about his other wife?” I ask him with a sneer. “You know, just as a precaution?”

He must be shocked that I would say anything. “I was brought up to speed with the other wife, and I can say that all requests have been denied. Her account is now frozen, and we will be requesting the funds be transferred to you.”

“What?” I whisper. “You’re taking her money?”

“Well”—he closes the folder—“it’s half Eric’s so…”

“No,” I snap. “I don’t want it. Cancel whatever paper you submitted.”

“Well, it seems that Mr. Schneider is in charge of that.” I smile as he says that, and I’m pretty sure I look like I’m losing my mind.

“I don’t give a shit,” I say, getting up. “I don’t want anything that he had with that woman, not one fucking penny. So you can either listen to me, the executor of his will, or I can get another lawyer.” My hands are opening and closing. “I think her finding out that her husband wasn’t her husband and that everything they had was a lie is enough, don’t you think?”

He just leans back in his chair as he looks at me, and I continue, “I mean, she filed for his insurance papers and those got denied, right?”

“They got denied because the case was fraudulent since he used his middle name and the information he used to apply wasn’t truthful,” he tells me, crossing his hands on his desk. “Mrs. Schneider, it is my duty to make sure you are taken care of, you and your children.”

“Stop the paperwork, Mr. Feldman,” I tell him, and he just sighs. “It’s enough, don’t you think?”

“Fine. I will pull the complaint, but it may be too late.” He takes off his glasses.

“Well, if it’s too late, I want to know how much you got, and we are going to reimburse her. To the penny.”

“Very well,” he says. “I will have to let Adrian know about this.”

I shake my head. “Do what you have to, but what we discussed here isn’t to be discussed with him.” I don’t wait for him to say anything. Instead, I walk out the room, down the hall, to the elevator, and make it to my car before I yell out in frustration. I pitch my purse to the side, grabbing the keys.

“Fucking asshole,” I say out loud, slapping my hand on the console. “Great fucking plan, Eric. Fuck not only me but the other woman by leaving your father to go after her. Fucking awesome.” I shake my head, turning on the car and pulling out of the parking lot. I stop at Wal-Mart on the way home, grabbing chips, soda, and nail polish—everything I need for the night. I smile at the clerk who wishes me a good day.

I look at my phone, seeing it’s almost time for the kids to be home. I send Judy a message.

On my way home. I’ll get the girls.

She just answers back one word

Okay.

That is it; only one fucking word. I stare at the phone, waiting to see the bubble with three dots reappear. I wait and wait and get nothing.

I put the bags into the trunk when my phone rings. Seeing a weird number, I contemplate whether to answer it.

"Hello?" I say, holding the phone with my shoulder while I close the trunk and push the cart back.

"Samantha." The voice makes me stop walking in the middle of the parking lot. A man honks at me, telling me to move. "Hello?" he says again. His voice smooth, his voice soft, his voice somewhat comforting.

"Blake?" I ask, but I will never forget his voice. From the first moment he explained who he was to the time he sat in my kitchen with his cousin, his voice will always be familiar.

"Yeah," he breathes out. "Listen, I know that the last thing you need is for me to call you, but"—I turn and walk back to the car as I listen to him struggle to find the words—"I just wanted to check and see if you were okay."

"What?" I whisper; this man who doesn't even know me, who knows nothing about me, who has met me a total of one time, not counting the wake, is asking if I'm okay.

"I've been thinking about you since we left you, and I know that Crystal can come off strong and I just," he starts saying and then stops. "So, I was just making sure you were okay."

"I don't think I will ever be okay," I say, getting in the car and making my way home. "I'm sorry," I tell him.

"For what?" he asks, surprised.

"I just left the lawyer's office, and he told me that they froze your sister's account," I say as I park the car in front of the kids' school. "It wasn't me."

"We know," he says, and I sit here a little stunned. How does he know?

"How?" I ask him. From this day forward, I'm asking all the

questions and getting all the answers.

"Because I know," he says, and I smile.

"You don't even know me. You know nothing about me," I tell him, looking at the kids starting to come out of the school.

"You're right, I don't, but I know you enough to know you aren't the vindictive type. You don't want to cause my sister any more pain than necessary. You want your life, and you want her to have hers."

"We sat at the table for five minutes," I tell him, getting out of the car. I wave to the girls when they walk out of the school, smiling when they see me.

"It was in your eyes," he says softly. "Someone holding that much pain doesn't want to inflict it on someone else."

"My kids just got out of school," I tell him.

"I'll let you go. Take care, Samantha," he says, and he disconnects before I can say anything else.

Chapter Nine

Blake

I shouldn't have called her. I shouldn't have called her. I stare at the phone that I just disconnected. I shouldn't have called her, but I couldn't not call her. I had to make sure she was okay.

Her eyes haunted my dreams all night. The pain, the emptiness, the sadness—it was just too much.

"Hey." I hear from behind me, and I look up to see Ricky. "Someone is outside asking for you," he says, and I get up, walking to the front. I'm in my squad uniform of blue pants and a blue t-shirt. I walk downstairs, coming face-to-face with Rosanna.

"Hey," she says, smiling at me. "I brought you lunch," she says, holding up a brown paper bag. Rosanna is or was Frankie's best friend.

I smile at her. "This is a nice surprise." I kiss her cheek. "Let's go sit outside." I put my hand out to lead the way.

"I figured since I was in the neighborhood, I would stop in," she says, sitting down at the table we have set up outside. I open the bag, taking in the two meatball subs that she got for us.

"Good thing we came outside. Not sure the boys would be

able to sit by while I ate this," I say, biting off a big piece.

"I figured." She smiles and takes a bite of her own. "So what's new?"

I shake my head, grabbing another bite. "Nothing much. Same old, same old."

She nods her head. "Yeah, I was afraid of that," she says as we finish eating in silence. "It's almost her anniversary," she says, and I nod. In one month, she will be gone seven years.

"Yup, crazy it feels like just yesterday," I say, thinking that the pain is still there, still lingering on the surface. Not a day goes by that I don't think of her, that I don't close my eyes and see her face, that I don't picture her smile.

"She would kick your ass," Rosanna says. "Kick it from here to wherever if she knew you were living in the past."

I roll my eyes at her. "I'm not living in the past."

She crosses her arms over her chest. "Really?" She shoots up an eyebrow. "When was the last time you went on a date? When was the last time you smiled at a woman? When was the last time you …" She doesn't finish, she just throws out her arms and widens her eyes. "You know"—she leans in—"had sex?"

I throw my head back and laugh. "I don't like to date, and I also don't really have time. Plus, I smile every single day. Sometimes at women, and sometimes, I even give them a nod and a chin up."

She shakes her head, rolling her eyes. "And I'm not answering that last one." It's been almost seven years since I made love to someone, since I held someone, since I was with someone. I know hookups can be easy; trust me, I work with enough man whores to know it can be just about sex, but I can't put myself out there.

"You're basically a monk, which is sad since you're so hot." She pushes away from the table. "I have to go, but we will be revisiting this conversation next month." She leans up and kisses my cheek. "Stay safe," she says, turning around and walking to her car. I clean up our mess, tossing everything in the garbage. I jog upstairs to the kitchen and find everyone just lounging around while we wait for a call.

The night goes by quietly with no calls, and most of the guys head off to bed. I grab my phone and go to sit down to watch television, but my phone rings as soon as I sit down. I look at the time and see it's almost eleven. But that doesn't shock me as much as the name on the phone. Samantha.

"Hello?" I answer softly and quietly because some of the guys are watching a movie.

"I'm so sorry; are you sleeping?" she asks in a whisper.

"No, I'm at work," I answer, going into an empty room. "Are you okay?" I ask her at my regular volume.

"I'm fine," she says, not whispering either.

"Why were you whispering?" I ask her.

"Because you whispered," she answers, and I laugh.

"Well, then, now we can have a normal voice conversation," I tell her, "but it's late. What's the matter?"

"How did they meet?" I close my eyes and lean my head back. "We were having a girls' night, and my kids watched *Tangled*, and the whole time, the only thing that I kept thinking about was how did they meet."

"Samantha," I say.

"I need to know," she finally says as I hear the rustling of her covers. "I have no family." She cuts me. "No one." I don't even know how to answer her. "I was an orphan, a ward of the state. Never had a father, never had a mother, I never had a family."

"Samantha," I hiss out with the need to reach into the phone and hold her.

"So I met Eric while I was waitressing. I fell really quickly;

he was everything I wanted in a man. And his family accepted me with open arms."

"Why wouldn't they?" I lean back in the chair, seeing her in my head.

"Well, they were my family. They are my family. But…" She stops talking, and when I hear her sniffling, I know she's crying. "But now I don't know anymore. It's just the more I ask them or shoot down Eric, the more they are pushing me away."

"Assholes," I hiss, thinking about his brothers and how different it would be for her if she was a part of my family, and I stop in my tracks.

"So now I'm here, and I'm questioning everything. I have so many fucking questions, and the only person who can answer me is buried."

"What if I don't have the answers? What if no one has them?"

"Then I go on, but I need to make some sense of what he did. I need to know if I was the one who pushed him away. I need to know that no matter what I did as a wife, I didn't fail."

"Fuck," I hiss. "Who the fuck put that shit in your head?" I ask angrily, so fucking angry I think the phone is going to snap in my hand.

"No one." I know she's lying. "Just, can you help me?"

I close my eyes while pinching the bridge of my nose. "What do you want to know?"

I hear her covers rustling again. "Before we do this, you need to promise me that whatever you tell me is the truth, no matter how much it may hurt me. I'm not searching for half-truths. No more. I need to know even if it hurts, even if I get mad, even if it's not what I want to hear. I need to know."

"Jesus." I shake my head. "You can't let sleeping dogs lie?"

She now laughs out loud. "He's dead, so I'm not sure he gets a vote."

The sound of her laughter fills my body with something, making me smile. "Okay, fine, what do you want to know?"

"How did they meet?" Simple enough.

"He was in town, I think working, and they ran into each other when he was walking out of the restaurant, and she was walking in."

"Figures," she says under her breath. "How long did they date before he proposed?"

"Shit," I say, trying to think. "I'm not really sure. I want to say nine months, maybe a little bit more."

"Did you like him?" she asks me.

"Very much. He was a brother I never had. When he was home, that is." I stop myself. "I don't mean home. I meant when he was here. His home was with you and his girls."

"Thank you," she says softly, "but I don't even think he knew where his home was."

I'm about to say something else when the alarm rings. "Shit, I have to go. We just got a call."

"Oh," she says quietly, "okay. Thank you for this, Blake." She disconnects, and I run out of the room, getting my gear on as we are briefed about a kitchen fire that just started in a house. The owner came home from work and fell asleep with the oil on the stove. It's two hours later when we pack up all our gear and head back to the station.

Shrugging my jacket off and stepping out of my gear, I pull my phone out of my pocket and see that I have a message. It came in right after we hung up.

Thank you for tonight. Stay safe.

I look at the time, and see that it's almost two in the morning.

Anytime.

I answer her back, and I'm shocked when she answers right away.

Glad to know you're safe.

I don't answer, thinking maybe I woke her up, so I close my phone and head to the shower and then quickly crash once I'm done.

I dream of Frankie, I dream of the time she told me she loved me, I dream about the time we sat on the beach watching the water with her in front of me. Her hair blowing in my face. But when I lean down to kiss her, Frankie's face doesn't smile back at me. It isn't Frankie's lips I lean down to kiss—it's Samantha's.

The next day, I try to forget the dream while also trying to make sense of it. I try to convince myself it's because she needs help, because she's alone. But when I open the phone and text her, it isn't about Eric, and it isn't about Hailey, it's about her. It's about making sure she is okay.

I hope you are having a better day.

I press send and put it back in my pocket. I'm getting up and getting something to eat when it buzzes in my pocket, so I pull it back out.

I'm actually having the best day in a long time. Thank you for asking.

I smile, putting the phone away. That night, I don't know why I expect my phone to ring, and I don't know why I constantly check the time. I don't know why I'm disappointed when I see it's eleven thirty and no calls have come through. But then, my phone rings.

Chapter Ten

Samantha

I shouldn't call him. I shouldn't want to call him, but he holds the answers.

After I hung up the phone with Blake last night, I lay in bed thinking about what he told me, thinking about the questions I still needed answered. I turned and drifted off to sleep but never fully fell asleep, so when the phone beeped at two thirty, it was no surprise who it was. I answered him and quickly fell back asleep because the morning would be here way too soon.

The girls and I got up and made pancakes together, hung out in our pjs all day while we watched every single Disney movie we had. We ordered Chinese food and ate in the living room; the mess was very minimal, but I didn't care one bit. Even when half the box of rice fell on Daisy and went between the cushions, I just shrugged. I cleaned up the mess while they showered, and now we were all camped out in my king-size bed. And it was fucking blissful. I watched the time go from nine to ten to eleven and then finally caved. I picked up the phone, sneaking out of my bedroom and going downstairs. He answered after one ring.

"Don't you sleep?" he asks instead of saying hello. I laugh.

"I took a three-hour nap today," I tell him, and it's the truth. The minute they put on *Boss Baby*, my eyes closed, and I slept till the end, and even was asleep when they put on another one.

"Figures you didn't even sleep last night," he tells me, and I hear the softness in his voice. "Did my text wake you?" he asks, the worry evident in his voice.

"We aren't allowed to lie, right?" I ask him. "Yes, you did."

"Sorry," he says. "I should have just waited until this morning."

"It's okay," I tell him, and it really is. "What do you do?" I ask him. I'm not sure if he's a police officer or fireman.

"I'm a firefighter for the county," he says, and the job fits him.

"So you do shift work?" I ask, not sure how it works.

"Yes, we do shifts. Four days on, three days off," he answers, and I hear creaking in the background.

"Is it hard?" I ask, not even able to imagine being gone from home for four straight days. "What happens if you have a family? A wife and kids." And my heart stops for just a second. Holy shit, he could have a wife and kid, and I'm calling him, I'm texting him. "Are you married?" I ask before I even know the words are coming out of my mouth.

"So one question at a time," he starts. His voice just soothes me, so I lie down on the couch with the phone tucked between my shoulder and my cheek. "It is always hard; sleeping on a cot is nothing like sleeping in your own bed."

"This is true," I agree with him. "Although I have to say I hate making the bed. I don't really ever make it. No, that's a lie," I say right away. "I don't want to make it, but I do."

He laughs, and I smile. "Usually the wives pass by or they go home for an hour or so. They do it in shifts in case something happens," he answers, and then I hold my breath, knowing it's the last part of the question. "I'm not married, nor do I have children."

"I should have asked that right away. It wouldn't have been right for me to call you and text you if you did," I tell him quietly. And then I realize what I said. "I mean no disrespect."

"I get it," he says, breathing heavily. "At no time did anyone suspect he was married," he finally says out loud. "Not fucking once."

"I think I knew," I whisper. "I mean, I didn't know, know, but …" I finally breathe. I've never told anyone this, not even Judy. "He had just come back from being away for two weeks, and he came in and just kissed me on the lips and turned around. No hug, no I missed you, nothing."

"Okay," he says, waiting for more, and I give it to him.

"I felt him pull away. He turned, hugged the girls, and gave them attention, then took off to take a shower. Lizzie looked at me confused, like she didn't understand why he wasn't hugging us, why he wasn't telling us how much he missed us and that it was so long and he hated it. There was just something missing. I chalked it up to him just being tired. He was just …" I feel my arm get wet with the tears that are coming now. "I dismissed it and told myself it was nothing. Till the next time it happened, and I waited until after the kids were in bed and went down to him as he watched television. I turned off the television and asked him if he was happy." I laugh bitterly. "He was very quick to tell me that he was more than happy."

"Samantha."

"No, it's okay," I say. "I told him that if he wanted out, he could go, and I wouldn't stop him. I would never stop him. I would never ever keep the girls from him. I begged him, Blake, fucking on my knees begged him to tell me." I sniffle. "I sat there giving him the fucking out, and he got off the couch and sat in front of me and held my hands, telling me he was just tired, telling me that he loved me more than life itself, telling me that the girls and I were his life, and that without us, he wouldn't be able to survive," I say. "After that, he made an effort, but it was never the same, so I sat there waiting each time he came home to tell me he wasn't happy, to tell me he was moving on, but then I got pregnant."

"Samantha," he says quietly, but I don't stop.

"I sat on the toilet and begged for it to be negative, prayed to whoever would listen to me for it be negative. It wasn't; it was positive, and he was so happy, or at least, that is what it felt like. And then two days later, the cramps started, and I woke up covered in blood. I knew what was happening. I knew that somehow I actually wished our baby away, and they took it." I don't even try to stop the sobs.

"Samantha," he whispers, and I feel like he is so close. I feel like he is here holding me, and he isn't. "These things happen."

"I know," I say, my nose stuffed. "I know it was a sign, but I can't help but think I wasn't the only one who didn't want it. I wasn't the only one sending out that prayer." I wipe my tears. "Did they want children together?"

He blows out. "Yes, every single time they were together, they talked about it. They were going to start trying next month."

"What would he have done? How would he have been a father to that child and my children? How do you have two lives?"

"I don't know, Samantha," he says. "I don't think anyone can answer that. I have to believe that one day, both worlds would have come crashing together, and he would be out two amazing women."

I whisper, "I wonder if he loved me." I blink, my eyes getting heavy. "I know he loved me, but was he in love with me or was I just there?"

"You're killing me," Blake says.

"I'm tired," I finally say. "I think I'm going to go to bed. Thank you, Blake. For this, for listening to me, for answering me." I don't wait for him to answer. I just hang up the phone and drag myself to bed, cuddling into Daisy. I close my eyes, letting the blackness take me to sitting on a beach watching the waves crash to shore like where we went on our honeymoon. I feel his arms around me and look back to kiss him, but it isn't Eric. Those blue eyes are green, the clearness now cloudy, and the smile belongs to Blake.

The next morning, we are all up at the same time. The girls sit around the table, and I'm opening the fridge when the doorbell rings. I walk to it and open it to see it's Elliot. "Hey," he says. "I brought doughnuts and figured I could visit with the girls."

I step aside as he walks in. He's never, not fucking once, rang that doorbell. He has a key and has used it ever since we moved in. "Did you forget your key?" I ask him.

"Nah, I just didn't know if …" He stops talking, not sure what to say. "It's been a weird couple of days."

"Has it?" I answer him, putting the doughnuts on the table while the kids get up and run to him, telling him all about our girls' weekend.

"Are you not going to Mom and Dad's for Sunday lunch?" he asks me while the kids are eating.

"I'm not sure," I say. "It got a little tense the other day, and I don't want to step on anyone's toes."

"You're family." He smiles at me, and I look at him and shock him when I answer.

"Families take care of each other. Families hold and support each other, not watch one of their own being shoved down and beaten."

"Sammie," he finally says, "I should have …"

"Yeah, you should have, but you didn't, so I get it. I'm really not family; I just married into it. My mistake.”

“Girls, do you want to stay home or go to Grandma and Grandpa’s?”

Daisy yells that she wants to go, while Lizzie says that she would rather just stay home. I look at her, not sure what is going on.

“Why don’t you take Daisy?” I tell Elliot. “And Lizzie and I will stay home and relax.”

He nods at us. “Sure thing. Sugar plum, go get dressed so we can go.”

I watch Daisy run up the stairs while Lizzie leaves the table to go upstairs to her room. “Dad is going to wonder why you aren’t there.” Elliot looks at me.

“Okay.” I shrug my shoulders. “Tell him I wasn’t feeling well. Tell him Lizzie didn’t want to go.”

“Sammie, he was just mad.”

I slap the table, angry now. “He fucking blamed me for Eric marrying someone else. Like if I would have fucked him seven days a week, it would have stopped him from going out and seeking someone else.”

“It wasn’t like that.”

“How?” I throw up my hands. “How wasn’t it like that?”

He doesn’t have a chance to answer because Daisy comes skipping into the room.

“Ready freddy,” she says.

“Give mom a kiss,” Elliot says, and she turns and comes to me, kissing my lips.

I walk them to the door, then wave at them as I watch them drive away. I close the door and then head upstairs, not expecting what is to come.

Chapter Eleven
Samantha

I knock on the door to Lizzie's room. Opening it up, I find her sitting on the middle of her bed, closing the book she was reading. "Hey," I say to her. Walking into the room, I take a seat on her big queen-size bed. The room is straight out of a magazine. She and Judy set out to create her own private oasis.

The bed sits in the middle of the room with her name painted in the middle of the wall. It took them two days to finally put everything in its place when Adrian went on a business trip. A desk is in the corner with a funky lamp on it, piled with her stuff.

"You okay?" I ask her, sitting on the bed in front of her. "You are acting awfully weird."

She looks down and then back up at me, the tears so big in her eyes they run over. "Baby." I reach out for her, but she shakes her head.

"I know, Mom," she says, and I look at her with my eyebrows pinched together. "Is it true?"

"Is what true?" I ask her, sitting up straighter as my heart beats faster and faster and faster. "I don't know what you're talking about."

"Who is Hailey?" My mouth snaps open as I watch my baby girl sit in the middle of the bed struggling to understand anything in this fucking mess that Eric left behind. "Mom, was Dad married to another person?"

I reach out for her hand, holding it in mine. "Baby, this is just …"

"I heard it all," she says finally. "I heard Uncle Elliot and Uncle Ethan talking in the garage. He married another woman." Her body not able to contain her sobs. "He didn't love us anymore."

I grab her in my arms as her sobs rip through her, hating him at that moment. I hate him for giving her this burden, I hate him for giving her this pain, I fucking hate him. "He loved you with everything he had. Everything." I smooth her hair down. "He loved you so much, so, so much; all he did was for you."

"So then why would he marry someone else?" It's the million-dollar question.

"Honey." I look in her eyes as tears fall down my face. I want to take away all her pain. "Your father loved you and Daisy with everything he had. Never ever, ever doubt that." I kiss her cheeks. "We were going through a tough time; it isn't anyone's fault. He fell in love with this lady."

"How?" she asks. "How do you love so many women you marry them?"

"I don't know. I can't answer that," I tell her honestly. "I have no idea, not one. The only one who can answer that is Dad."

"Would he have tried to take us with him?" she asks with fear. "Would I have had to go?"

"Honey, all these what-ifs are going to make you sick. The only thing we have to remember is that he loved you so, so much."

"I'm angry with him," she says. "So angry." She looks down.

"I'm also angry with Grandpa A."

"Why are you angry with him?"

"He was mean to you two nights ago and said some mean things. I don't want to talk to him."

"I'm a big girl. You don't have to be mad at him for me. He loves you."

"And I love you," she says.

"Now, I want you to promise me that you won't tell anyone you know. Promise me that if you need to talk, you come to me, and I will answer any questions you have honestly, even if it hurts."

"Okay, Mom," she whispers. "I won't tell anyone." The last thing anyone needs to know is that she knows. "Can we go watch a movie?" she asks, and I smile. "*Beauty and the Beast*."

"Cartoon or real?" I ask her, not really caring. I could do both.

"Real." She smiles, climbing off her bed. "I'll start the movie, and you get the doughnuts."

I smile at her. "Meet you downstairs in a bit. I have to go to the washroom." I walk into my room as Lizzie walks downstairs to get the movie ready, waiting till the door closes before letting my sob out. If I didn't hate him before, I fucking hate him now. Leaving our children with doubts of how much he loved them. He was a selfish, selfish, selfish bastard, and I hope he's somewhere rotting.

I wash my face, then head downstairs to Lizzie. We end up watching the real and then the cartoon version when Elliot brings Daisy back.

Daisy crawls on the couch with me, kissing my cheek and lying down on my lap. "She should pass out soon. I took her to the park."

I look down, bending to kiss her nose while she watches the end of *Beauty and the Beast.* "Did you bring any leftovers?" I ask him, and he looks down and then up again.

"No, Mom didn't cook that much." I just nod my head, knowing full fucking well it's a lie; my mother-in-law cooks for an army. "She cooked less 'cause Dad is going away for business."

"That's okay," I tell him, and he stands there awkwardly. I don't say anything else. Instead, I turn to watch the movie.

"I'm going to head out," he says, and I turn, smiling at him.

"Have a great week," I tell him as he comes to kiss the kids goodbye.

I wait for the door to close, then turn to Lizzie. "What do you feel like for dinner?" I ask her as she just looks at me.

"We can have pancakes"—she smiles—"with chocolate chips."

We make pancakes together, side by side, as we dance to songs that Lizzie chooses, and Daisy runs around, dancing on one foot. I put the kids to bed, kissing them and telling them I love them.

I take a shower, looking at my body in the mirror. I've lost a good fifteen pounds; my hipbones are sticking out, and I hate it. I grab my pjs, putting them on, and then going around the house, making sure everything is locked up.

I get into bed and turn on the television, flipping through the channels. Looking down at my phone next to me, I pick it up and call him.

He answers after two rings; groggy, his voice is rough. "I'm so sorry. I didn't know you were sleeping. I'll call you tomorrow."

"Hey, you," he says, and I hear the rustling of his covers in the background. "I got off shift today, and I usually nap, but I guess I was more tired than I thought. How was your day?"

"Eventful," I say softly, turning on my side. "Are you sure you don't want me to call you back?"

"Nope," he says. I don't know why, but I picture him in bed, his black hair sticking up everywhere. "How was it eventful?"

"Lizzie knows about Hailey," I say softly, and that wakes him up.

"What?" he asks with a madness to his voice. "How?"

"She heard Ethan and Elliot talking in the garage, and well, she had a boatload of questions."

"I bet she did. I'm old enough to understand, and I have a shitload of questions."

"I had to sit there, holding her and telling her that he loved her more than life while the whole time I cursed him and hoped he was rotting in hell."

"I don't think you are the only one wishing that," he says, laughing.

"My in-laws are boycotting me," I say, and I don't know why I tell him. "We got into a fight the other night, and well, let's just say I'm no longer feeling the love," I say as my thumb rubs the underneath of my eye.

"What happened?" he asks, and I contemplate telling him the truth.

"I was pissed that they were going after Hailey's bank account, and I voiced my opinion. Well, let's just say if I was a proper wife, he wouldn't have looked elsewhere." Just saying it out loud makes me see how stupid it sounds.

"Who fucking said that?" His voice is loud and almost screaming. "I swear to God."

I laugh at him. "It doesn't matter. I know it's a crock of shit. What hurt was that no one stuck up for me. No one came to my side; no one told me that it was bullshit. No one took my side; no one held my hand and said he's crazy." My voice goes soft.

"I'm sorry. Where was Elliot or Ethan?" he asks.

"Sitting at the table," I tell him. "Was he involved with your family?"

"Yes," he says, and I know it hurts him too now. "My grandmother loved him, and my mother considered him another son. When he was in town, we all knew because my mother would have a dinner."

"Did he hold her hand?" I think back to when he stopped holding my hand; I think back to when it started to change.

"Every single chance he got."

"Maybe he did love her more than me," I say, thinking about it. "Maybe she was it for him."

"He was a coward. No man would do that to someone they love."

"Have you ever been in love?" I ask him, waiting for him to answer.

"Yes, I have," he says softly, "and I'll love her till my last dying breath."

"So why don't you marry her?" I ask him.

"Because she died and left me when we were twenty."

I sit up as his words hit me. "Oh my God, Blake, I'm so, so, so sorry. That was insensitive of me," I tell him.

"You didn't know, so you had no reason, but if she was still here, I like to think we would have been married and had at least a couple of kids by now. Frankie always wanted a big family," he says, and I can sense a smile fill his face.

"I'm sure she would," I say, yawning. "I'm going to get going. I'm sorry I woke you," I tell him. "Sweet dreams, Blake," I say, disconnecting. Lost in my own thoughts, I'm jealous of the love he had for her. Jealous that no one ever loved me so fiercely. Not once.

Chapter Twelve

Blake

"Sweet dreams, Blake," she says softly and then disconnects. I lie here, waiting for I have no idea what. For her to call me back, for her to text me. I get nothing.

Getting up, I make my way to the kitchen, grabbing some water and then heading back to bed. I fall fast asleep as soon as my head hits the pillow. My dreams don't bother me tonight, and I wake up right when the sun rises. I grab my bag and make my way to the gym. I do mostly cardio since we have weights at the fire station. When I finally walk out of the gym, it's almost nine o'clock, so I send Samantha a text.

Hope you are having a better day.

When she told me about her in-laws last night, I wanted to get in my car and drive over there and beat the shit out of every single one of them. Who doesn't hold their family up? Who doesn't fucking support and care for the mother of your grandchildren?

A text message comes in, and my phone pings

Fingers crossed, hoping that you have the best day!

I smile and then pull up in front of Hailey's house. Walking in, I see Hailey sitting in the middle of shattered glass with roses all over the floor. The card right in front of my foot shows me that they are from Eric.

I grab the broom, sweeping up the majority of the mess while I watch my sister in the chair, crying. I wonder what would happen if this was Samantha. I wonder who would hold her, who would be there for her. The answer is no one. How sad is that?

So lost in my own thoughts, I don't hear the door open nor do I see Nanny come in and take a look around. She says nothing when she sees the garbage with the roses in it. Instead, she shows Hailey a picture of a house on the beach. She goes on and on about her friend Delores who has a house for rent, and how this is what Hailey needs.

"She just can't leave," I say as Nanny looks over at me.

"And why not?" I try to answer, but Nanny doesn't even give me a chance to. "She has nothing here. Nothing. Yes, she has her family, but she needs to find herself. Staying here in this museum she calls a home isn't helping anyone. Besides, she works from home. All she needs is her computer, and she is good to go."

"Yes." The sound comes out in a soft whisper. "Yes." Hailey looks up as Nanny smiles, and I scratch my head. How in the hell is her moving away from her family a good thing? I try to make eye contact with Hailey, but she is too fixated on the picture of that house.

"I want to have a yard sale." Hailey looks at me. "I want to sell everything. I want nothing." I look around her house, seeing all the touches of Eric, and know this purge will be painful for her, but hopefully, it helps her heal.

"I'll make the posters today." Nanny gets up and walks to the door. "I guess this is like that song 'Cleaning out the Closet.' Remember, Blake? You used to sing it each day in the mirror, wearing your white t-shirt and your jeans hanging low under your ass." She laughs. "Until I told you that inmates wear their pants like that to have …" She cups her mouth with her hands and whispers, "Butt sex."

Hailey snorts as I throw my head back. "Oh, good God," I groan as Nanny walks out of the door. I look at my sister. "You sure you want to go there all by yourself?"

She doesn't get a chance to answer because Crystal walks in. "Hey, you guys," she says, tossing her purse on the couch and coming in to start the coffee. "Whatcha looking at?" she asks as she picks up a picture of the house. "This is so pretty."

I fill her in. "That is where Hailey is going to, as Nanny says, 'find herself.'" I use my fingers to make air quotes.

Crystal and I look at each other while I open the fridge and take out the ingredients to make breakfast. Hailey starts making a list of what needs to be done. I don't say much except when she asks for a real estate agent, I pick up the phone and call Sophie.

Sophie and I went to school together, and she promised to come by this afternoon to see her.

I walk out of the house and climb into my truck. The phone rings, and I don't know why, but my heart speeds up just a bit when I see her name.

"Did he cook dinner?" she asks when I answer. Her voice is different, not sad but as if she is asking whether you want fries or a salad.

"Umm, it would depend, but usually yes."

"Asshole," she says, and I laugh. "He never fucking cooked."

"Can I ask what brought this on?" I pull into my driveway.

"I hate deciding what to cook for dinner. It just feels like it's always the same thing."

"Tacos," I tell her, and she gasps.

"On a Monday?" She laughs. "Living on the edge."

"That's me, the badass." I laugh, getting out of the truck.

"Were you in the car?" she asks as I hear pots banging in the background.

"Yeah, I just got home. Hailey is leaving," I say, sitting on the couch now while I talk to her.

"What?" she asks softly. "Why?"

"According to Nanny, she needs to find herself and doing it moping in the house and getting drunk isn't it."

"She gets drunk?" she asks softly, and I hear sniffling. "Is she okay?"

"No," I answer honestly. "Not even close, but I'm really hoping that she will be."

"Where is she going?" she asks me, her voice picking up just a bit.

"Some house on the beach. We are selling everything," I tell her. "Cleaning out the closet."

"I wish I could do that," she says. "I have all his clothes still hanging in the closet, and I don't even bother opening it anymore."

"When it's time, you will," I tell her.

"Did you live with Frankie before she died?" she asks me.

"No, we were planning to, but she fell sick right before we could," I say softly, remembering. "Our goal was to move out the minute we both could afford the down payment. I had just joined the academy, and she was starting her nursing program."

"How long were you two together?" she asks with a laugh.

"Five years," I say. "We met our first day of high school."

"First love," she says, and I quickly correct her. "Only love."

"I have to go get the kids," she says, and we both say bye and disconnect.

I get up, making my way to the kitchen, not hungry anymore. I lie on the couch and flip on the television. Finally deciding on a movie, I let my mind spin while it plays. I keep thinking about the questions she asks; I keep thinking of the doubt she must be going through.

My phone beeps on my chest, and picking it up, I see it's a picture from Samantha of her hand holding a taco with the caption.

Queen of the badass.

I laugh at her, thinking it's one small step for her, but I know it's a huge one.

I send her back a reply.

Lock the doors, there is a badass on the loose!

She sends me back a simple:

hahaha

I put the phone down as I continue watching the movie, but my mind isn't on the movie; it's on a table some two hours from me where three girls try to fix their broken hearts. She doesn't call me that night or the night after.

On my first shift back, I sit on my bunk, wondering if I should call her. I don't think any more because my fingers have already dialed. She answers after one ring.

"Hey," she says, and I smile, listening to her voice.

"Hey, yourself. Did the taco police take you hostage?" I ask with a smile on my face, and she laughs softly.

"Very funny," she says, and I hear rustling.

"Were you in bed?" I look back at my watch, seeing it's nine.

"I was," she says quietly. "I took another step yesterday."

"Oh, yeah?" I ask, my interest piqued.

"I called Elliot and Ethan and asked them if they wanted any of Eric's clothes." I think I stop breathing, listening to her. "Needless to say, it didn't go over well."

"What do you mean?" I sit up in my bed, my blood starting to boil. That whole fucking family needs to be knocked on their asses.

"Well, there were lots of questions, and then some guilt about erasing him from our lives," she says as she sniffles again. "How the fuck am I erasing him from our lives when I have his two children?" she asks, and I don't think I've ever hated someone more in my life. "Like I don't get it."

"Why didn't you call me?" I'm not sure why I ask that question. I'm not even sure we qualify as friends.

"Because I thought you've heard me bitch enough over the past couple of days."

"Oh, please." I roll my eyes. "Asking me questions and discussing tacos isn't bitching."

"Tomorrow, I'm painting the house," she says cheerfully.

"Are you?" I ask, wondering if her brothers-in-law will help her.

"I am. The girls and I discussed it, and we are going to do one room at a time," she tells me, finally a pep in her voice. "We are starting with the kitchen. I wanted a soft yellow; is that a weird color?"

"Soft yellow?" I ask.

"Yes, I was researching on Pinterest, and it's so pretty and uplifting, the color like the soft sun. Besides, no one frowns when they see yellow. It makes you smile."

"Does it?" I tilt my head, smiling. "Was that on Pinterest also?"

"No, that was on Google when I searched for the most cheerful color." She laughs, and I shake my head with a chuckle. "I'm not kidding."

"I would never doubt a woman and Google," I tell her. "Ever."

"Did Eric do things around the house?" she asks.

"Yes," I answer. "But in his defense, Hailey always started it when he was gone, and he would finish it for her."

She pffts. "Meanwhile, for him to cut the grass, I had to cheer him on." Her voice isn't sad this time; it's kind of the opposite.

"Okay, so yellow kitchen and then what?"

"No idea," she answers. "One room at a time."

I shake my head. "You really are a badass."

She laughs now, a full belly laugh. "It feels good," she says, "being a badass. Or maybe it's you."

"Me?" I ask her, but she can't answer because the siren sounds. "Gotta go." I disconnect, getting myself downstairs while I get into gear. It's only four hours later when I check my phone and see she sent me a message as soon as the call came in.

be safe.

I look at the clock and see it's way past one a.m. I'm afraid to wake her up, so I make a note to message her tomorrow. I fall asleep, dreaming of nothing but yellow—yellow sun, yellow sand, and blond yellow hair.

Chapter Thirteen
Samantha

I wake and check my phone to see if he texted me back while I kiss the girls good morning and head downstairs to start breakfast and make coffee.

I yell for the girls, and we rush out, catching the bus without a second to spare. When I get back home, I get in my car and hit up Home Depot. I go straight for the paint department, choosing a soft, soft yellow. I pick up everything I need in order to make it happen. I walk to the car with a smile, unloading the car in four trips. I'm finally moving things out of the room when the doorbell rings. I walk to it, seeing it's Judy.

"Hey," I say, opening the door. "Come in."

She comes in, smiling, and follows me to the kitchen. "Sorry, I can't offer you anything. I'm about to start painting."

She gasps out in shock as she looks around and sees the mess of the room, the yellow paint poured in the pan in the middle of the room. "What are you doing?" she asks, looking at me.

"I'm painting the room," I tell her, thinking it's pretty obvious as to what I'm doing. "It's been a long time, and it hasn't been painted, so why not?"

"Well, Eric painted this room two years ago," she says, wringing her hands. "It's just …"

"I've been asking him to paint this room for a year, and he never did it," I tell her, picking up the roller. I roll it in the paint and then try it on the wall to see how the color looks. "Isn't it pretty?" I smile, turning to her and seeing her scowl.

"No, actually, it's not." She folds her arms across her chest. "It's ridiculous."

I shrug my shoulders, not letting her get to me, but the tears start coming as I blink them away, or at least try. "I like it."

"This whole thing has gone on long enough," she says, her words coming out in almost a yell. "Ever since Eric died, you've changed. It's like you aren't even that person anymore," she spits out, and I turn around, looking at her.

"I think you seem to be mistaken on that." I look at her, my heart pounding and almost breaking when I see the look she is giving me, the look like I'm an afterthought, the look she'd give a stranger. "You see, when Eric died, my entire life came out as a lie." I blink, and the tears still fall. "Everything that we had for the past twelve years has been playing in my mind."

"He made a mistake!" she shouts.

"A mistake?" I laugh and cry at the same time. "A mistake is he chose the wrong shirt to put on, or he picked up Coke instead of Diet Coke." She glares at me. "Marrying another woman wasn't a mistake. Living with her for eighteen months wasn't a mistake. Painting her house and fixing up her house wasn't a mistake. It was a choice. A choice he made because he was selfish."

"How do you know he did all that?" she asks, and I just shrug.

"I'm assuming since he didn't do them here, he must be doing it somewhere."

"Well, that's the problem; you're assuming instead of knowing."

I shake my head. "Well, he slept with her, he had sex with her, and he promised to love her forever. Am I to assume he didn't mean that?"

"Maybe if you had stopped harassing him when he was home and had been more understanding, it wouldn't have led to that." And I'm gutted; I'm so fucking gutted I don't even think I can breathe. Her hand flies up. "Maybe if you had been there for him and caring to his needs, he wouldn't have gone elsewhere."

I step back. My chest is heaving, rising up and down as if I ran a marathon. It's almost broken; my heart is broken as I look at this woman standing in front of me who pretended to love me. "So Eric doing what he did was all my fault?" I ask her, and she doesn't answer. "No!" I yell now. "It wasn't my fucking fault that I was a single parent for the past eighteen months while he was off gallivanting and making himself another family. Without you guys, might I add." I rub the tears off my face angrily. "It's not my fault that he felt the need to lead two fucking lives. That's on him." I shake my head. "Now I'm here by myself raising two girls, trying to make it look like we can live without him. I'm trying to give them the normal that they need, that they deserve. That I finally deserve."

"You were nothing before Eric." And it's at that moment I know she never loved me; she never cared for me. She never felt I was a part of her family.

I smile at her as I cry and break inside. "Wow, boy, was I stupid. Here I thought when you said I was just part of the family that you actually meant it, that you meant you loved me no matter what. That it didn't matter what happened before because now I had you guys. You were right about one thing; I was nothing before him, but I'm something now. I'm a mother now. They are my life; they are my family. They are mine."

"We'll see about that," she says, and she storms out of the house, slamming the door behind her.

I look at the paint, and nothing comes in me, not one piece of happiness is in me while I look at the paint. I take my phone out and send Blake a text.

I might be rethinking painting the room yellow.

I don't know why I sent him a text. I don't even know why I'm sad he doesn't get right back to me, but I look back at the wall and see the yellow. It's a change, and it's my house. I look at the mess of the kitchen, turn around, and take a deep breath. Dipping the brush into the paint again, I continue to paint. The more I paint, the more I feel a little happier. Until the phone rings and when I walk over with a smile, it immediately disappears when I see that it's Elliot.

"Hello?" I say.

"What the fuck did you do to Mom?" he asks right away, anger in his voice.

"I didn't do anything to *your* mother," I tell him.

"She just called me, and she is hysterical," he hisses.

"She came to see me and saw that I'm painting the kitchen. According to her, it's my fault that Eric cheated and married someone in secret," I say, putting the brush back into the paint.

"I doubt she said that," he says.

"Of course, you do, because according to your mother, I was nothing before Eric, so I mean, I can't expect anyone to believe me or actually be on my side."

"Sam," he says quietly now. "She's going through a lot."

"Really, you don't say?" I laugh. "I mean, it's not like I lost my husband, and then my girls lost their father, and I lost the only family that I've ever known. I'm sure she is going through a shit ton."

"I just think you should relax when you talk to her."

"How's this? I won't talk to any of you since every single time I try to tell you guys how I feel, you just feel the need to let me know how perfect Eric was," I say, finally sounding defeated as I just hang up on him.

I sit in the middle of the kitchen now, my legs crossed, looking around and seeing my little piece of happiness. I sit here, thinking about how the last time we painted the kitchen, he bitched the whole time—his shoulder hurt, he hated the color, he was tired. And I walked around on eggshells, trying not to piss him off. I had to take the kids to the park just so he could have peace and quiet.

My phone rings again, and this time, it's Blake.

"Hey," I say, smiling.

"Sorry I didn't text you back. I had to save a cat."

I throw my head back and laugh. "What do you mean?"

"I mean, the fucking cat went into this tree and wouldn't fucking come down, and then when I finally got to the fucker, he hissed at me and bit me." I can't stop laughing while I picture him in a tree chasing a cat. "Luckily, I had my gloves on, but yeah, so why isn't yellow a good idea anymore?"

"My mother-in-law came in when I had just started painting."

"Oh, fuck," he says. It's funny how he's never really met me, and he doesn't know any of us, but he knows it's bad.

"Yeah, well, it went downhill," I say softly. "I think what hurt the most was when she said I was nothing without Eric."

Blake hisses, but I continue, "I grew up a child of the state, so I'm used to all the names. But I figure in twelve years, I loved your son and had his children, which are your grandchildren. I think I'm someone."

"You're more that someone," he tells me. "To those girls, you are the world. You're showing them that you live even when it's hard. You're showing Lizzie that you can be sad and then dust yourself off and survive."

"You think so?" I ask him. "Do you know I don't even know what Eric's least favorite color was."

"Green," he says right away. "He fucking hated green."

"Fuck," I say and laugh. "I wanted to paint my bedroom his least favorite color, but green …?"

He laughs now. "Yeah, I don't know about that."

I look at the clock. "Shit, I gotta get the girls," I tell him. "I'll call you later." I disconnect and run to the bus stop, getting there at the same time as the bus pulls up. The girls and I walk back to the house, and I know right away I made the right choice because my girls love the new kitchen.

So all the doubts are gone when I get to see the smile on Lizzie's face as she does a circle in the room and her eyes light up. *Totally worth it*, I decide as I smile to myself and not once do I think about Eric.

We end up making grilled cheese for dinner while I finish painting, and when it's finally done and everything is put back into place, I take a picture and send it to Blake with the title, My Sunshine.

I put my phone away and smile as I fold my arms across my chest and take in what I just did, and by myself, no less. I smile the whole time I walk upstairs and take a shower and then smile even bigger when I see that Blake has sent me fifteen Pinterest ideas for a green room.

I call him as I get into bed. "I think you should go with mint," he says softly when he answers.

I laugh. "Well, if I have to pick between the moss green and the mint, I would pick the mint."

We talk about our days, and I tell him how happy the girls were when they came home. "See, you hang the moon to those two."

"If you could change one thing in your life, what would it be?" I ask him when we both yawn.

"That we found Frankie's cancer earlier," he says without skipping a beat. "What about you?"

"That I found out about Eric before he died," I say softly, and we are saved by the bell when he leaves for a call and disconnects.

Chapter Fourteen

Blake

"I can't believe we sold everything," Hailey says to me as she puts her bag in the front seat of her car, and I follow with her two suitcases, putting them into the trunk. In the past week, she has donated Eric's clothes to the homeless shelter, sold her house, and had that yard sale where she sold everything except Eric's tools. She gave those to me under protest—I didn't want them—but then I thought about who I would give them to, and I knew that it would be only right to give them to Samantha. If she didn't want them, she could give them to the girls.

Samantha, who like Hailey, is trying to purge Eric from her system, has single-handedly repainted her whole house. After her kitchen, she painted her living room. That conversation still makes me laugh.

"I'm moving on to the living room, and I think I'm going to take the picture of us down," she said late one night, later than usual since I was out on a call.

"Did you talk to the girls about it?" I asked her as I lay in bed thinking about her in her own.

"Not yet," she answered with a yawn. "I'm going to take it

down to paint, and we can talk then."

"What color did you choose?"

"Well, according to Google …" She laughed as I closed my eyes and silently laughed. "Muted blue is the coziest color."

"So yellow kitchen, blue living room. Mint green bedroom."

"It sounds like a Skittles commercial," she said laughing, something that she did more and more. I smiled at her, and then she hit me with another one of her questions.

"If you could change one thing in your life, what would it be?" She's asked that same question every night before we hang up.

"That I didn't marry Frankie when I wanted to," I said without missing a beat. "What about you?"

"Not following my gut," she said softly. "Good night, Blake," she said and hung up.

I looked at the ceiling as I thought about how she was doing with no family and no support; she literally had no one. Not one person except her girls. The burning in my stomach set in; if I ever got five minutes alone with his brothers, I would pound the shit out of them. Good thing my father was a lawyer.

The next day, she painted the whole living room a soft blue, and it looked fucking awesome.

Shutting the trunk, I snap out of my memory. Hailey comes to hug me around my waist. "What am I going to do without you?" she asks me as tears start to form in her eyes.

I smile down at her. "You know I can be there in eight, maybe seven hours. Just call and I'll be there." She nods her head and then is taken aback when Crystal arrives and informs her of what we all knew. There was no way she would let Hailey go without her.

Hailey turns to us, letting us know she is going to do one last walk-through of the house and wants to do it alone. We both look at each other as she walks up the stairs, and I turn to lean back on the car.

"You guys going to be okay?" I ask Crystal as she leans next to me.

"I think so, but it all depends on her." Crystal shrugs her shoulders. "She decides she wants to come back, we come back."

"What about your job?" I look over. Crystal shrugs her shoulders again. "Will you tell her about Samantha?" I hold my breath.

"Yes"—she puts her head back—"when she's ready." We look up then as she comes out of the house with tears streaking her face. Crystal rubs her arms while she goes to the driver's side door, leaving me and Hailey alone.

"Here is the key." She hands me the key to the house. "The real estate agent will stop by the firehouse at three p.m. to pick it up." I grab her around the neck and pull her to my chest where she sobs.

I hold her and comfort her till she steps away. "How did you do it?" she asks me, and I know she's talking about Frankie.

"Don't do what I did. Don't shut yourself off from the world. Live," I tell her honestly, only now regretting some things I've done. "Promise me you'll live." She smiles as she places her hands over my hands on her cheeks. "You have to listen to me. I'm older," I tell her, and she laughs.

"Yeah, yeah," she says to me as my hands leave her face, and she nods. "Promise me the same." I nod this time, putting my hands in my back pockets as her blue eyes stay shaded and protected.

"Get out of here," I say to her as I walk back to my truck. "See you next month for sure." She nods at me, climbing in the passenger side. I watch the car drive away before turning and making my way to the station. Walking in, I check in with the captain, who is getting up to get his coffee.

I pull out my phone and send Samantha a text, not sure what time she gets up.

Today is going to suck.

I don't expect her to text me back, and she doesn't. Instead, she calls me, the sleep apparent in her voice. "It's too early to know that."

I laugh, grabbing a cup of coffee for myself. "I just feel it."

"Does that mean I should paint the bathroom before going green in my room?" I shake my head at her, smiling. "You know what color came up when I Googled?" she asks me, giggling, and I turn the sound up then as that was the best thing I've ever heard.

"No idea," I say, thinking maybe red.

"Seafoam green." She laughs out loud, like belly laughs, and I have to laugh with her. "Fucking seafoam green."

"There it is, painting the bathroom green," I say. "He would hate it."

"See and you said today wasn't going to be a good day. Lies," she says, and I hear a little voice, "Mommy, I'm up."

"Come here, baby girl." It's the first time I've heard her talk to her kids, or that I've heard the voice of them.

"My alarm just rang," she says, and I hear kissing and then giggling. "A blue-eyed monster just put her cold feet on me." She laughs, and then I hear her again. "I'm not a monster; I'm Daisy."

"You're right; it's going to be a good day," I tell her as she disconnects and goes to do her mom thing. She sends me a picture ten minutes later. It's the first time she's sent me a picture of herself, but it's really not of her, it's of a coffee cup in front of her lips, hiding what looks like a smile, her eyes cut off. I laugh when I see what the cup says,

'It's a great day for a great day.'

I text her back right away.

You might be right. Happy painting.

The rest of the day goes by so fast, we have four calls, one car accident, and then another fucking cat call. I don't even see my phone till it's way after eight, and I see that I have a couple of messages. I open the first one from Crystal.

I need you to go to Nanny's house and kill her. This fucking house is nothing like the picture, nothing.

I laugh and then click the picture she sent me of inside, and I gasp. I message her right away.

Come Back Home.

I check my second one from my father.

Can you come over this weekend and help me in the shed please?

I answer that one also with two words.

Roger That!

Then I see Samantha has sent me five messages, and I laugh when I scroll through them.

There is no nice seafoam green.

I even tried to combine two greens. Looks like snot.

I can see why he hated green.

I'm buying it anyway.

Then she sends a picture of her hand on a paintbrush while she paints the wall.

I guess it isn't that bad, if you're Shrek.

I laugh and then call her.

"Hey," I say when she answers, and I hear yelling in the background. "Where are you?"

"I'm at the park. Elliot called and wanted to see the girls. So I brought them to the park."

"Are you with them?" I ask her.

"Nope, I'm sitting by myself while they run around the playground."

I picture her sitting on the grass all by herself with the sun shining as her blond hair moves. "How is the painting going?"

She laughs now. "According to Daisy, we should only do one wall, and I agree with her wholeheartedly. What about you? Was your day better?"

"Yeah, Hailey moved today," I tell her, and she says nothing. "Is it weird talking about her?"

I don't see her smile, but I hear it in her voice. "You mean weirder than talking to my dead husband's fake wife's brother!"

I laugh. "Say that fast ten times."

"The kids are yelling for me. I'll call you later," she says as she disconnects. I look at the phone, and I'm not sure what to think. I'm not sure what is going on, and I don't have time to think about it because another call comes in.

This time, it takes two firehouses to put out an apartment building up in flames. By the time we get back to the house and shower, it's too late to call her, and I see she tried to call me twice.

She sends a message.

Going to bed. Hope you're okay.

I close the phone and head to my cot where I dream of every single color of green. When I get up in the morning, I'm so fuck-ing happy it's the last day of my shift. I get up and look at my phone and see that she hasn't called me. So I call her and it goes straight to voicemail. I don't bother leaving a message, and by the time I get home, she still hasn't called. I'm going to be hon-est—she's got me worried. I wait till it's after nine and try again.

I call her back, and this time, she answers. Gone is my bubbly girl, and in her place is the devastated person she was before.

Chapter Fifteen

Samantha

"I really hope they sleep well after that," I tell Elliot as we walk home from the park. We, or better yet, he just spent two hours running around the park with them.

"It's good to see them," he says as Daisy and Lizzie walk in front of us. "Daisy's getting so big."

"No one is stopping you from seeing them," I tell him. "I would never do that to them. Family is very important to me."

"I know Mom and Dad miss them also."

"So then why haven't they called them? Why haven't they shown up to see them?" I ask him as we slowly walk back. I try to keep my voice down so they don't hear me.

"It's just that they don't feel welcome anymore."

"Well, that's on them, not on me. I painted the house, for Christ's sake. I didn't change the locks."

"I know, but it's just a big change for everyone."

"Yeah, don't I know it. We used to have dinner with you guys four times a week, and now you go days without calling me. Your mother and I used to go do mani and pedis every single Thursday, and now I'm sitting waiting to see if she will call."

I don't get to finish because we finally get home, and the kids start to run inside. "Come say goodbye to Uncle Elliot," I tell them.

We make our way upstairs, and Lizzie takes a shower while Daisy takes a bath, and by eight thirty, they are both snoring.

I collapse in bed, also calling Blake, and it goes to voicemail. I wait an hour and then call him back, and I figure he's on a call, so I send him a text.

The next morning, I start my routine by walking the kids to the bus stop. Today my goal is to clean out Eric's closet. It's random and spur of the moment, but I think I'm up for it; I think my heart can handle it. I open the closet, and his woodsy smell hits me right away. It's almost as if I'm letting him out. I can't explain it. His smell is all around me; I feel him all around me. I don't think I can do this after all, but my hand moves without me realizing what is going on. My fingers going to his shirt, a shirt I washed and ironed for him. I flick it off the hanger and fold it, putting it on the bed, and I go to the next one, and by the time I look around, all his clothes are folded on my bed. I get two plastic bins out and stack the clothes in them, putting them in the corner to be carried downstairs.

I grab a stool and grab some of his shoe boxes from on top of his shelf. When I take down four, I step off and put them on the bed. Opening them, I see the shoes are almost brand new. "I don't know why he bought so many fucking shoes when all he wore were his Nikes and his steel toe boots."

I get back up and pull the next stack down, finding a brown plastic bag on top. I open it up and see pictures of the kids along with a woman's watch. The card is with it. *Happy Mother's Day to the best mom ever*, he wrote, and a tear comes down my cheek. It's two months away, yet he knew what he was getting me.

My finger traces his writing, and I bring it to my chest.

I get back up and take the remaining shoe boxes out. A brown envelope in the corner under the boxes slips off the shelf with the boxes. It lands on its back, and I bend down to pick it up. My name is written on top, so I flip the flap open and pull out two folded white pieces of paper. I open and see it's a letter from Eric, and my legs give out. I fall with my back against my bed as I read his letter.

My sweet Sammie,

I don't know where to begin, so I guess I'll start at the beginning. When I first saw you waiting tables while I studied for my final, something inside me shifted or clicked into place; I can't really explain it. All I knew was that I was mesmerized, and then you spoke to me and you literally sounded like an angel. Then when I asked you out, and you said yes, I thought I had won the jackpot, and in a lot of ways, I did.

When I watched you walk down the aisle, I knew I would never love anyone as much as I loved you. I promised to love, honor, and cherish you for all the days of my life.

I lied, and there is no easy way for me to say this. But somewhere between pledging my love for you and creating our two beautiful girls, I lost myself, or so I thought. I was going through the motions. Work, home, kids, repeat. It was as if the movie was just looping through, and I started to feel lost.

Then one day, I ran into someone, and the spark returned. I know this is a fucked-up way to find out, and if you're reading this, then something really bad must have happened to me.

But I married someone else. I honestly just thought it was an affair until I realized I couldn't let her go. I couldn't picture my life without her, but then I couldn't let you go either.

I'm a selfish fucking bastard, and I wanted you both.

I want to say I regret it, but I can't because loving you made me, but loving her completed me.

I hope that in time you can forgive me, that you can tell the kids the good about me, that you can protect them when the bad comes. You're stronger than you think you are.

With love always

Your Husband

Eric

The letter slips from my hands as does the envelope, but the pictures that are inside slip out, showing me who this woman is. Showing me who Hailey is. It's a picture of them on their wedding day. The wail that comes through me fills the house, and if the windows were open, I'm sure someone would have called 911.

I fall sideways as my body curls into the fetal position. I cry for the man I met, I cry for the man I fell in love with, I cry for the man who married me, I cry for the man who gave me two children, and I cry for myself because with one letter, he has left me more broken than I was before.

That one letter has shown me what was right in front of me the whole time; he loved me, but I wasn't good enough for him.

I lie in the spot as I hear the phone ring and ignore it. I only get up when it's time to get the girls, and no matter how hard I try to hide it, the kids notice.

"Are you sick, Mommy?" Daisy asks when we walk in the door, and I take off my sunglasses, the redness in my eyes giving me away.

"I'm just sad today," I tell her as Lizzie gives me a hug.

"I can make us nuggets in the toaster oven," she says and then turns to Daisy. "Get your homework, I'll help you."

I lie on the couch motionless as I blink and look at the picture that I still haven't hung back up. The picture I won't hang up. When it's bedtime, I roll off the couch and tuck the girls in and then come back to my room. The brown envelope is out of sight tucked under my clothes in the first drawer.

I close my eyes and rock myself, hoping that the darkness takes me, but it doesn't, no matter how hard I squeeze my eyes. When the phone rings again, this time, I reach out and answer it.

"Hello?" I say, my eyes closed as tears pour out onto the pillow.

"What's the matter?" Blake says right away. "Are you hurt?"

"Not that you can see," I tell him.

"Where are you?" I hear him moving around.

"I'm in bed," I tell him.

"Are you sick?" His voice is trying to be calm, but he's failing.

"No," I answer, and then I tell him, "I cleaned out Eric's closet today."

"Oh, shit," he says. "Why?"

"Because I thought today was a good day, because I thought I was strong enough, because I thought I would be okay."

"Where are the girls?" he asks, and I cry out a little bit because he doesn't even know them; he's never fucking met them, yet he cares more than their actual family does.

"In bed. Lizzie made dinner," I tell him. "He left me a letter," I finally say. "A confession of sorts. He told me all about Hailey. Also left me a nice picture of the two of them on their wedding day."

"Prick." I hear him hiss. "Why didn't you call me?"

"Because it happened so fast. I didn't even know what it was till I opened it. He loved her," I say with a sob. "Loving me made him but loving her completed him."

"I can't fucking believe this," he says. "I have to go."

"Okay," I say, hanging up as I look at the wall. I don't know how long I lie here; I don't know how much times goes by. The phone ringing snaps me out of it. "Hello?" I say quietly, seeing it's now a little past eleven.

"Open the door," he says and disconnects. I sit up in bed, shocked and surprised. I go to the front door and open it, my eyes taking him in. His green eyes shining in the moonlight, his blue shirt fitting him like a glove.

"What are you doing here?" I ask him, shocked that he is standing on my doorstep.

"I figured you needed a friend," he says, and I crush my face into his chest and cry out while he holds me.

Chapter Sixteen

Blake

I didn't even know what I was doing, but the only thing on my mind was getting to her. To her soft voice, her silent sobs, her broken spirit.

Gone was the woman who fought so hard and took so much pride in painting her house, and in her place was the woman who was left behind to feel she wasn't worth it.

It took me an hour and forty-five minutes to make the two-and-a-half hour drive. When I pulled up, the house was black. I didn't know if she would answer, didn't know if she was even up still, but I knew deep in my soul that she needed to know someone cared. Someone was going to hold her hand. She answered after one ring and her voice was much the same as it was two hours ago.

"Open the door," I tell her, and I disconnect. I stand here waiting to see movement. I don't at first, and then I hear soft footsteps coming down the stairs. The lock clicks on the front door, and ever so slowly, I see her. Her pink pj top goes off the shoulder with matching pants. Her brown eyes puffy from crying.

"What are you doing here?" she asks me, shocked I'm standing here.

"I figured you needed a friend." I smile at her, and she doesn't say anything; she just crushes her face into my chest. My arms go around her, the wetness of her tears soaking through my shirt. I pick her up in my arms and walk inside. Sitting on the couch, I cradle her in my arms, rocking her as she cries.

"I gave him everything," she says, grabbing my shirt in her tiny hand. "I gave up everything for him," she says quietly so as not to wake the girls. "My dream job," she says as her sobs soften and her breathing hiccups. "I was a social worker," she says with her head tucked into the crook of my neck. "I was going to make a difference, even if only to one child. I was going to do my best to make a difference." I'm so tempted to kiss her head, so tempted, but I don't. I just listen to her. "But then I got pregnant with Lizzie. I was so happy, and I didn't think I could be any more in love with another person in my life. The moment they placed her on my chest was overwhelming; it was everything. Eric was the one to tell me perhaps I should stay home. It would be better for her, so I did it. I left my job, but I got to spend every single day with my girl. Then Daisy came, and it was an overabundance of love. My heart grew tenfold, and I thought I was on top of the world. I thought it just doesn't get better than this. And then to be told that I just wasn't that up to par for him." She stands. "That I was just okay, but Hailey was the one who completed him." She lifts her head to look at me, and I want to hold her face in my hand and wipe away the tears. I want to bring her lips to mine, but I know I can't. "I gave him two beautiful girls," she tells me. "They are so beautiful."

"They are," I agree with her. "Just like their mom."

"How didn't I know?" she asks. She's looking at me like I have all the answers in the world, but I don't.

"You trusted him and believed in him. This isn't on you," I tell her, my hands itching to touch her.

"I believed him. I believed that he was just as fucking complete as I was. Boy, was I wrong." She shakes her head, standing in the middle of the huge room. I finally see her with the moonlight streaming in, and her face is fuller. It isn't sunken in. Her eyes, even though she has been crying, are different.

"When was the last time you looked in the mirror?" I ask her, the question surprising her.

She opens her hands in front of her. "I have no idea."

"Well, I suggest you do," I tell her, standing up. "I saw you less than a month ago, and you've changed." She looks at me, not understanding, so I grab her hand in mine. Our fingers fit almost perfectly. I push aside the feeling of her hand in mine and bring her to the kitchen with its sunny paint. I turn on the light and look around. "It was dead before," I tell her. "The walls were white and dead, and now it's sunny and full of life." I release her hand and turn around. "This is your sunshine; you did this, and you did it for your girls." I take a picture of the three of them with yellow paint on their hands off the fridge. "Look at the girls. You did that, not Eric." I don't stop there. I grab her hand and lead her back into the living room. "This," I tell her, "you're living, you're doing what he isn't. You're fucking living, and you're doing it, telling him to fuck off. You're doing it for your girls; don't let him win that. Not again."

She looks at me after she looks around. "You made a home for your girls; you gave them this. Not him. So it doesn't matter what he says, it doesn't matter if you made him or that Hailey completed him because, in the end, you complete those little girls, and it's so much better than him." She nods her head like she finally gets it.

"I can't believe you're here," she says, smiling. "You came

all this way."

"I figured I could see up close how bad the seafoam green is." I smile at her, and she finally laughs.

"It's really fucking bad," she says. Grabbing my hand, she pulls me to the bathroom. She wasn't lying; it's horrible.

"Let me make some coffee," she says, leading me back to the kitchen. She makes a cup of coffee, giving me the cup she once sent me a picture of. I sit here for the second time in my life, but this time, it's different. This time, I'm not here for Hailey; I'm here for Samantha and only her. She sits next to me with something in her hand. "I need to choose a color for my bedroom," she says, and for the next hour, we laugh over paint shades while she checks Pinterest for ideas. For two hours, we do nothing but talk about her bedroom, not one of us bringing up Eric. When I finally walk out of the house and head to my truck, I wave back at her. As I pull off, the phone rings, and the Bluetooth picks it up.

"Hello?" I say.

Her voice comes out softly. "I figured you could use some friendly conversation while you drive home," she says with amusement.

For the next two hours and a half, she tells me stories of what a horrible cook she is. How she once made meatloaf, but it was so soppy it looked like meat soup. I laugh as I tell her stories about the recipes that I do know, which aren't much. When I finally pull up to my house, it's almost five a.m. "Are you going to go to bed now?" I ask her.

"No," she tells me. "I think I'm going to make a big breakfast, and then when the kids leave, I'll go to bed." She yawns.

"Okay, call me when you wake up," I say, getting out of my truck and disconnecting. I take off my shoes, fall on my bed, and sleep for six hours straight. Getting up when the alarm rings, I walk to the coffeemaker, pour a cup, and drink it with my eyes almost shut. After taking a shower, I head to my truck and drive over to my parents' house.

I knock on the door then walk in and see my mother in the kitchen, taking out an apple pie from the oven. "Guess I'm here right on time," I tell her. I kiss her cheek and grab the coffeepot to pour myself a cup.

"You look tired," my mother says, putting down the oven mitts.

"Yeah, I had a rough night," I tell her and don't go into more detail.

"Anything you want to talk about?" she asks me, and I just shake my head. "Well, you know that if you need to talk about anything, I'll be here."

"I know, Mom." I smile at her. "Where is Dad?" I ask, looking around.

"He's in the shed already," she tells me, so I walk out to the backyard. Going into the shed, I hear him curse. Through the open door, I see him trying to get a shelf to stay in place.

"Guess I came at the right time," I tell him from the doorway as I hold up one side while he tries to nail the other side. I grab the hammer from him and push him aside so I can nail it in and it doesn't fall on his head. We spend two hours putting up shelves and fixing the one shelf he put up crooked.

When we finally finish, he looks over at me. "There is a reason I went into law." He smiles. "Because I fucking hate this shit." He takes off the gloves he has on to prevent getting a splinter in his hands. "You look weird," he says to me. "Something is off."

I shake my head. "Nothing is off with me."

"It's in your eyes," he tells me, and I look down at my feet, not sure what the fuck is in my eyes. He doesn't say anything; he just walks out, and I follow him.

When we walk in, Mom has lunch ready for us. "Your sister is in love with the beach," she starts telling me while I take a bite of the sandwich she made for me.

"I heard from Crystal that it's going well," I tell them. "Looks like everyone involved is finally moving on." I don't catch the words before they slip out, and I know for a fact my father caught it, but he doesn't say anything when I look up at him. He just gives me a sideways look and then looks to see if my mother noticed. She didn't, so I take another bite and pay more attention to every single word that comes out.

I finally leave after Mom wraps half the apple pie up for me. I pick up my phone that I left in the truck and see that Samantha sent me a text.

Did I dream that you came here?

Chapter Seventeen
Samantha

I roll over to check the time, and it's almost time to go get the girls. I get out of bed, dragging my legs to the bathroom. The shower only wakes me halfway. Going downstairs, I find the mess I left after breakfast, and I smile when I see the two coffee cups in the sink. He really came here. He really showed up for me. I grab my phone and text him

Did I dream that you came here?

I put my phone on the counter as I load the dishwasher and take some chicken out for dinner. I walk to the bus and am greeted by the girls and their big smiles when they walk off the bus.

"Mommy," Daisy says as she runs to me, arms outstretched. "You feel better?" she asks when I gather her in my arms, kissing her nose.

"Yes, I feel all better," I tell her, holding my arm out for Lizzie to join us. I pull her to my side and kiss her head as we talk about their day at school. We come into the house, and everyone starts their task, as I call it. Lizzie sits at the table and takes her homework out, something she's started doing lately. Usually, she would do it in her room. Daisy sits next to her, and Lizzie helps Daisy with her homework too.

I start dinner, putting the chicken in the oven while I make rice. "Did you guys want corn or peas on the side?" I ask them as I look inside the freezer, swaying to the music in my head.

I glance over my shoulder at the girls and see Lizzie smiling at me, shrugging her shoulders. "Either is good." She turns back to her homework. Daisy doesn't have a preference either.

Lizzie sets the table while Daisy puts the forks on the table and the glasses. When we sit down to eat, I look at them. "This weekend, how about we go to the park, and I can take some new pictures of you two to hang in the living room?" I wait to see if one of them will say something or notice. "I think two pictures of you guys hanging on the big wall will look so nice."

Lizzie looks up at me. "Yeah." She then looks at Daisy. "We could wear matching outfits and then we can even do one together to hang in the middle."

"That sounds like a plan," I say, smiling, and we finish eating while Daisy talks about what she wants to wear. I tuck Daisy into bed, then head to Lizzie's room last.

"Goodnight, love." I bend to kiss her head.

"I'm glad you're not sad anymore," she says. "I didn't like yesterday. I didn't like you crying."

"I know, baby, and I'm sorry." I sit on the bed. "It was just a bad day."

She nods at me, then sits up next to me. "I'm sorry you were sad," she says, hugging my neck. I kiss her and tuck her in. As soon as I get into bed, my phone rings.

"If you tell me to open the door, I'll really think I dreamed it." I laugh, and I hear his laughter in return.

"Nope, I'm tucked into bed," he says, and I wonder what his house looks like. I wonder if it's your typical bachelor pad. Does he have pictures on the wall? Is there a picture of Frankie by his bed?

"Tired?" I ask him as he yawns. "What did you do today?"

"I helped my father hang shelves in his shed." He laughs. "It's a good thing he's a lawyer because I swear the shelf was leaning with one side a good one inch lower." I laugh at how he describes the shelf and how when he put something on it, it literally slid down to the other side.

I laugh the whole time, my cheeks hurting from the story of his father almost smashing the piece. "I'm taking the kids to the park tomorrow," I tell him. "We are going to take pictures to hang in the living room."

"Really?" he says, and I hear the blanket rustling in the background while he probably flips over. "Well, that's a step in the right direction."

"Yeah," I say. "They didn't even ask where we will put the other picture."

"What are you going to do with it?" he asks me.

"I might just store it in the attic or ask maybe my in-laws if they want it." I take a deep breath. "Do you still have pictures of Frankie?"

"Yup," he says. "Right next to my bed is a picture of the two of us a week before she found out she was sick."

"I'm sure it's perfect." I smile for him. "Is that the only one you have?"

"Yes," he finally says. "I used to have them all over the house, but one by one, they came down. I don't need a picture for her to be part of this house."

"I never thought of that," I tell him, and it's true. "So besides saving your father from a nervous breakdown, what did you do?"

"I went to the cemetery," he says, and a tear slips out of my eye.

"Do you go there often?" I ask him, realizing I haven't been since Eric passed away.

"Every week," he says with a heavy breath. "Sometimes twice a week."

"Do you feel closer to her when you go?" I ask him.

"Sometimes. Sometimes, I swear I hear her bitch and tell me to leave and fuck off." He laughs, but I don't.

"I doubt that," I say softly. "I'm going to go to bed."

"What is one thing you would change?" he asks me for the first time.

"Not calling you sooner," I say. I'm not sure he answers or that I let him because I hang up the phone and tuck it away. My phone beeps, but I don't reach for it even though my hands itch to. Last night while I sat on his lap, I itched to reach out and feel his cheek, wondering if his whiskers would pinch my hands, wondering if he would smile when I did it. I wondered if he would stop me; I wondered if he would picture Frankie.

I close my eyes, not sure I want to wonder anymore. That night, I dreamed of sitting on the beach, but this time, I was by myself when someone I'd never met walked by. She was stunning, her long, dark curly hair being pushed back by the wind. She raised a hand to wave at me as she placed her hands to her mouth and yelled, "Go to him." I remember getting up and walking to her, but she disappeared as soon as I got close to her. I ran down the beach after her or what I thought was her, but then I came face-to-face with Hailey, sitting on the beach with tears running down her face.

Walking to her, I sat next to her, not sure if I should say anything, when she said, "I just want to be happy." I looked back at the water, then turned to look back at her, but she wasn't there anymore. My eyes flip open as the sun hits my face. I roll over in bed, looking outside. Daisy comes into my room and climbs into bed with me.

"I had a nightmare," she says as I raise my hand for her to come to me, and I cuddle her to my chest.

"It's okay. Mommy is here." I kiss her as her soft snores fill the room. I smile as her hair tickles my chin and fall back asleep with her. Lizzie climbs into bed with us sometime later, and we end up watching *Tangled* in my bed till their stomachs grumble.

I go back downstairs, and we make plans to go to the park. The girls are dressed in pink skirts and white shirts. We walk to the park with my camera bag over my shoulder and the girls skipping in front of me. My phone beeps in the back of my pocket. I still haven't checked it from last night.

I pull it out and find a text from Elliot.

Wanted to see if the girls were free to go to my parents' house.

I roll my eyes and call him instead.

"Hey," I say when he answers. "What's up?"

"My mom was wondering if the girls could come over for dinner."

"Just the girls?" I ask, and my heart hurts again, but this time, not that much.

He stutters, not sure what to say, so I let him off the hook. "It's fine. Listen, we are on our way to the park to take pictures, so I'll ask them and get back with you."

"I didn't mean anything by it. I just assumed you wouldn't want to come."

"It's fine," I say, "I get it."

I don't let him continue; instead, I hang up and ask the girls. Daisy is happy while Lizzie looks at the grass, asking, "Are you coming with us?"

"No, honey," I tell her. "I'm going to stay at home and relax." I lie to her as she looks at the ground.

"Okay, but not for long," she says, and I text Elliot back.

The girls said they would go.

He answers back.

Thanks.

And I wait for him to invite me, tell me that it would be good to have a family dinner, but nothing comes through. I see the message from Blake with his answer.

I would have come for you sooner.

I smile, putting my phone in my back pocket. Two totally different families, one who supports and loves unconditionally and the other who loves only when it suits them.

I take about two hundred pictures of the girls just enjoying themselves. Lizzie takes a couple of shots of me doing a cartwheel and laughing when I land on my ass. I get the girls home, and they go to change. When the doorbell rings, I open the door and see Elliot there.

"Hey," I tell him, moving out of his way so he can come in. "The girls are upstairs changing. Actually, can you come and help me?" I ask him, and he just nods. I walk up the stairs to the bedroom and point at the two bins in the corner. "Those are Eric's. I didn't know if you or Ethan would want any of them."

"Wow," he says, whistling, "you're really trying to erase him."

I stop dead in my tracks and turn around. "Excuse me?" I say, folding my arms over my chest.

"I thought Mom was exaggerating when she kept saying you're trying to erase him from the house. With the new paint, the picture of him down in the living room. His clothes packed. I guess she wasn't wrong."

I don't bother to answer him. I walk to the bedroom door, closing it and locking it. I walk to my dresser, and reaching under my clothes, I take out the brown envelope while Elliot looks at me. I open the envelope and notice a white one I didn't see before, but I push it aside and take out the letter he wrote to me. "Here." I shove it at Elliot, his eyes going big and his arms not moving. "Oh, don't you even fucking dare. This is a letter I found while cleaning out his clothes. A last letter from him." Elliot's face goes ash white. "Oh, wait, it only gets better. He made sure to include a picture of him on his wedding day to the woman who 'completes him.'"

He doesn't move, and I don't care. "Wait, I believe his words were 'I made him, but she completed him.'" I hold the picture up. "Would you like to see the happy couple?"

"That's enough," he says between clenched teeth.

"No!" I shout, "what's enough is you guys thinking I'm trying to erase him. It's called living. I'm fucking living." I raise my hands. "I have no choice because I have two girls who need me to live." I cross my arms now. "This is the last time we have this conversation. This is the last time you guys get to throw anything in my face. I didn't do anything wrong; Eric did." I take a deep breath. "I won't have you guys making me feel like I did something wrong."

"I'm sorry," he says as he looks at the picture in my hand. "Can I have the picture?"

"No," I tell him, putting it back in the envelope. "And if you want to read the letter, you can, but it doesn't leave my room."

"Mom." I hear Daisy knocking on the door. "The door is locked." I walk to it and open it.

"Sorry, it must have been stuck," I tell her. "Look who came, Uncle Elliot."

"Uncle E!" She runs to him. "We are putting new pictures up," she tells him after he throws her up and kisses her. Lizzie comes in, looking at the both of us.

"I don't want to go for long," she tells Elliot, who looks at her and then at me. "I have a book report due, and I want to finish it today so I don't have to do it tomorrow."

"Okay," he says, buying her excuse. "Let me load these bins in the car and then we can go."

I watch him carry the bins downstairs, and then I kiss the kids goodbye, waving at them from the door. I take my phone out when I can't see the taillights of his car anymore and send Blake a text.

Want to FaceTime me and have coffee?

Chapter Eighteen

Blake

She never answered my text, her words still lingering in my mind. The softness of it, day by day, a piece of us left behind. There are so many different things going on, and I am not going to sit and think about it. I'm not ready to.

The whole day, I cleaned the house and picked up shit. Packed away stuff. I was fixing the bed when she texted. I pressed Face-Time right away.

Her face fills the screen. "That was fast."

"I was making the bed," I tell her, laughing. "Just finished."

"Just in time," she says, smiling. "Did you eat dinner?" she asks, sitting at the kitchen counter.

"No," I tell her. "Did you? Where are the girls?"

"I did not," she says. "The girls were invited to my in-laws' house for dinner."

"Why didn't you go with them?" I ask her, watching her face. Her brown eyes light today.

"I wasn't really invited," she tells me, and I roll my eyes.

"I've never seen you annoyed before," she says, laughing. "It's okay, really."

"It so isn't okay. What the fuck is it showing the girls?" I ask her, and I see her eyebrows pinch together. "It's disrespectful not to invite you."

"Honestly, it's good to just be by myself," she tells me. "We spent the day at the park taking pictures." Her eyes light up. "I think I got some good ones."

"Really?" I ask her, and she gets the camera to show me the ones she took. "Is that you doing a cartwheel?" I ask, laughing.

"Yeah. I tried anyway," she tells me. "I gave Elliot Eric's clothes." She puts the camera down while she picks up her coffee cup and takes a drink. "It was a little tense there but …" She puts it down and comes closer to the phone, her face filling up the screen. "I showed him the letter. He wanted to take the picture of Hailey and Eric," she says, and the hair on my neck goes on alert. "I didn't let him take it or the letter."

"You did good," I tell her, not sure why it was the right move, or why it was a good idea not to have him hold it.

We chat for two hours when I hear the door open and the girls yell. "I'll call you back in a bit," she tells me, disconnecting, and I toss the phone to the side. I scroll through my phone, looking for Elliot's number. I'm so close to calling him and fucking telling him what an asshole he is, but I don't. Something stops me.

For the next two weeks, we continue our chats. More Face-Time conversations when the girls aren't around. On Friday, her face isn't the same. She looks worried.

"What's the matter?" I ask her right away.

She looks at me. "The girls are going camping with Elliot tomorrow for the night."

"Okay?" I ask her. "Do you not want them to go?"

"It's not that; I know he would never hurt them," she says. "It's just I haven't been without them overnight since before Eric."

"Do the girls want to go?" I ask her, wondering, and she nods.

"Even Lizzie is looking forward to it," she says, and I try to tell her that everything will be okay. "Yeah, yeah, I know," she tells me, and we quickly get off the phone.

I look at the phone and then up again, taking a pull from the beer I had on the table. I won't be talking to her tomorrow, and I haven't told her yet. I'm not sure I can.

The next morning, I wake up, dread filling me right away. I get out of bed, and for the first time, I don't look at Frankie's picture. I put on my jeans and get into the truck. The phone rings right away. Looking down, I see it's Samantha, but I don't answer. I send it straight to voicemail. Not today, I can't today.

I pull up at the cemetery with the bouquet of red roses on the seat next to me. I grab them and carry them with me as I walk to Frankie's grave.

"Morning," I say to the black granite stone that holds her name.

"I brought you flowers," I tell her as I place them down on the middle of the stone.

I sit down, bending my knees, and rest my arms on my knees as my hands hang. "Do you remember when I asked you to marry me?" I ask her and close my eyes, taking me back to the moment.

"I don't understand." I looked at her as she stood there in the middle of the hospital room, one frail hand holding the IV pole that she wheeled around with her when she walked. A blue satin scarf wound around her head where her beautiful, thick curly hair had been. In its place, she had patches of hair growing back.

"I will not marry you," she said with her head held high, the blue cotton robe hanging off her. She hadn't been well this whole week. No matter what we did, she couldn't fight the cold she was

coming down with. Her immune system was too depleted from her treatment.

"Do you not love me?" I asked her, with tears running down my face. I was on one knee in front of her with a ring, asking her to be my wife, to be mine.

"Don't do that," she said, not moving from her spot in the middle of the room while holding the red roses that I brought her in her spare hand. "Don't make this harder on me than it has to be," she said with tears running down her beautiful face. She had lost so much weight, her cheekbones stuck out now. She held her head high on her slender neck, so slender I was afraid to put my arm around her when we sat down.

"I'm on my knee asking you to be my wife, asking you to be mine." I begged her to give me this one thing.

"No," she said adamantly and then had to walk to the bed to sit down, her chest rising and falling in shallow breaths.

"Why?" I looked at her, taking in her face, knowing I would never forget this moment. There were balloons and a cake ready in the hallway along with all our family members and a priest. I wanted to marry her right away.

"Because you will only get married once in your life. It's just the way you are; you are loyal to a fault. If you marry me, you will never move on," she said with tears running down her face. "If you marry me, you will never marry anyone else; you will never have babies. You will die with me, and I won't do that to you."

"You think just because I put a ring on you and marry you that I won't move on? You think a ring is going to stop me from moving on?" I got up, mad that she wasn't giving me this. "You think regardless of if you marry me or not, that I'll move on?" I shook my head, the hurt coming from my stomach. "I don't want anyone but you," I told her.

"I love you with everything I have," she told me. "I love you enough not to hold you to the promise that you make me. I love you so much that I won't let you die with me. You have to promise me," she said, her breathing getting weaker. "You have to promise me that you'll live and fall in love."

The roses fall from her hand. Her hand goes to her chest, and I yell out for help. She closed her eyes and fell into a coma right after that.

The tears run down my face as I come back to now. Looking at the roses move in the breeze, I shake my head. "I can't believe you never married me." I try to joke with her, but the hurt is still here seven years later.

I close my eyes, and I'm back to that same day. *The balloons were gone, the cake out of my face. We sat by her bed as I held her frail hand in mine, kissing the inside of her wrist where her heart was beating. Faintly. The doctor had just left, and he didn't have to say what we all knew. There was nothing he could do. Her body was failing. Her parents sat on one side of the bed while I sat on the other, and the tears never stopped. "I love you," I whispered to her, and her eyes fluttered open.*

"I'm tired." She looked at me. "I can't do it anymore." She didn't have to tell us because we knew. We saw it in her eyes. "Best thing I ever did was join that debate team." She tried to be funny, but no smile came to her face. "Don't close yourself off," she told me. "Live."

"I love you," were the only words I could say.

"Then live," she said. "Do everything we said we would do. Promise me you'll fall in love."

"Frankie," I said as she closed her eyes, and then slowly opened them again.

"Promise," she whispered, and then closed her eyes. Two hours later, she took her last breath and took my heart with her.

My eyes slowly open as I look at what's left of her—the cold black stone. "I'm sorry I didn't do what you told me to." I lie on my side, resting my head on my arm. I sit here for what seems like forever, then get up and go to my truck. My phone is beeping from calls and messages. My family knows what today is. They give me my space but always call just to check on me and tell me they are here for me.

I see that Samantha has called a couple of times and has also left a couple of messages. *Not today*, I tell myself, though I'm not sure what that feeling is that creeps in.

I get home, close the door and all the drapes, and take the bottle of whiskey out of the cupboard on my way to the couch. I pour myself a couple of shots, taking them all in a row. The initial burning starts to slowly go away. For two hours, I finish the bottle. The sun's setting, and I close my eyes, hoping that the darkness takes me until tomorrow. I rest my head, and I'm about to sink into the darkness when a soft knock makes me open my eyes. At first, I think I've imagined it, that it's just in my head, but I hear it again.

I get up to go to the door when the knock sounds again. "I'm coming," I bark out and swing the door open. "What?" I say, and I'm not sure if it's the whiskey or my imagination, but she's standing there in front of me.

"I figured you needed a friend," she says softly, and right then, my heart fills for the first time in forever. Her smile fills me; it makes almost everything okay.

"How did you know?" I ask her, moving aside to let her in.

"I didn't," she says softly as she looks around. "The kids left for the night, and I went into my room and I read the letter again. But this time, this fell out." She takes the white envelope out with Hailey's name on it. "Seems Eric wanted to say goodbye to her also."

She turns around and notices the empty whiskey bottle. "Am I crashing a party?" she asks, and I don't know why, but I tell her.

"Seven years today, Frankie died," I say and then go to the couch and she follows me.

"Do you have another bottle somewhere?" she asks me, and I actually smile. "In the kitchen."

She gets up, and I follow her the whole way. She's wearing jeans and a sweater, nothing sexy, but she oozes class. She comes back with it and pours a shot in the glass and hands it to me "To a great, great woman." When she holds the bottle up, we click the bottle to the glass, and she takes a pull while I swallow the shot. She hisses. "That's fucking awful," she says, coughing, and I laugh while she pours another shot. I raise it to my mouth, but she doesn't join me.

"How did you know where I lived?" I ask her.

"I didn't. I went to the firehouse I found online. They gave me your address," she tells me and smiles. "FYI, they think I'm a stripper gram."

I burst out laughing, smacking my leg. "No way."

"I had to make it believable." She laughs as I swallow another shot. My vision starts to get foggy.

"I promised her I would fall in love," I say, looking at her sitting on my couch. "I lied."

"You'll fall in love again. I know it," she tells me, smiling with tears in her eyes. "Anyone would be lucky to be loved by you," she says, crouching down next to me and looking straight into my eyes.

"I can't love anyone. I'm broken," I tell her the truth. "Half of me is broken."

"What if you find someone who is just as broken as you are and"—she swallows, and her hand comes to my face as she cups my cheek in her hand—"together, you're whole."

My hand moves on its own, brushing the hair from her face. "I would be so lucky," I whisper, and then my eyes close, and the darkness finally finds me.

Chapter Nineteen
Samantha

I don't know what I was thinking. Fuck, I wasn't thinking. When the girls left, I went to my room and remembered the white envelope stuck in with the letter from Eric. When I pulled it out, I was in shock that he left Hailey a letter. I immediately called Blake, but he didn't answer. I knew he wasn't at work, and when he spent most of the day radio silent and then didn't answer my texts, I got worried, so I decided to take a drive. Was it my smartest moment? Obviously not. When I walked into the fire station, the eyebrows all raised when I asked if he was around. I joked around, saying I was his stripper, and one of the guys finally gave me his address.

When I knocked on the door, all the drapes were closed, but his truck was in the driveway. When he opened the door, the glaze in his eyes was apparent, and so was the shock of seeing me. I had no idea today was the anniversary of Frankie's death.

He's suffered all by himself; the big man with the biggest heart I've ever seen suffered by himself all day long. So I sat with him shot after shot until he passed out. But not before he told me he could never love again. Not before my heart broke for him and with him.

I close the door softly behind me as I walk down the steps to my car. I hold the tears in until I sit in my car and head toward my house. Our conversation plays over and over in my head for two and a half hours. When I finally roll home, I don't bother to turn on the lights. I just walk to my bedroom and kick off my clothes, the first tear finally falling. Of course, I went and fell in love with a broken man who could never love me back.

I fell in love with a man who thinks he's so broken he can't love another person. "Wow, do I know how to pick 'em," I say and fall into bed. The darkness comes for me easily, and the next day, when I roll out of bed, my whole body aches.

I walk to the coffeepot, and my phone rings, showing me it's Blake. I press connect to start the FaceTime.

"Did I dream that you came here last night?" he says. I look at him, and his face is rough this morning. I laugh at his one eye open and the other eye closed.

"Would it freak you out if I said it was a dream and you thought you were going crazy?" I laugh at him as he groans.

"I can't believe you came and just left," he says as he lays his head on his arm. "I woke up looking for you."

I shake my head, placing the phone down while I start the coffee. "It was a rough day yesterday," he says softly, and I go back to the phone. "It's been so long, yet it feels like it just happened."

"I guess when it's that day, the memories of what you did that day just suddenly surface, right? I mean, I can never smell lemon again without thinking of Eric."

"Yeah. I asked her to marry me the day she died," he says, and my heart breaks for him again. "She said no." He shakes his head. "Every single year, it's the only memory I have."I look at him, not sure what I should say. Not sure there are any words out there to say. "Anyway, thank you for bringing Hailey's letter. I'm going to visit her tomorrow when I get off my shift."

"That should be relaxing. You can detox all that whiskey from your body," I tell him, winking at him as the doorbell rings. "Okay, mom duty time." I hang up and go to the door, opening it for the girls.

Lizzie comes in and doesn't say anything but just goes upstairs. I watch her and then turn and look at Elliot. "What is wrong with Lizzie?"

"I guess she just didn't sleep well," he says, dumping their bags at the front door without making eye contact. "Um, I guess I'll see them around," he says and walks out. The whole encounter is so fucking weird.

I look at Daisy. "What in the world?" I ask, and she looks at me. "I don't want to live with Grandma and Grandpa either," she says, and then I call Lizzie right away.

"Come here please," I say, and she comes down the stairs with tears running down her face. "What in the world?" I take her in my arms, and she sobs. Her hands squeeze me so hard when my arms go around her. "What in …?" I whisper, and she finally lets me go.

"I don't want to go live with Grandma and Grandpa," she finally says out loud.

"Why would you think that?" I look at Daisy and then Lizzie.

"Uncle Elliot wanted to know if we would like to go live there instead of here," Lizzie says, and my heart stops and then beats faster. "When I got mad, he said it was just a question."

"I don't know why he asked you this," I tell them both, "but there is no way I would let you live with them when your home is right here. Now, let's unpack the bags, and we can have movie day on the couch." I smile, and they walk with the bags to the laundry room. I pick up my phone and call Elliot and it goes to voicemail. I call him back again and leave him a message. "Elliot, you need to call me back."

I hang up the phone, but my stomach never settles, even after we watch two movies and the girls return to normal. That night, I text Elliot when he doesn't call me back, and he doesn't answer that one either.

I toss and turn all night long, my hands shaking with nerves, and the next morning when I get back home from dropping off the kids, my phone rings, and I jump at it, expecting it to be Elliot, but it's Blake.

"Hey," he says, and I sigh. "What's up?"

"I'm waiting for Elliot to call me back," I say. Sitting down, I feel my legs shaking with nerves. "He asked the kids if they wanted to go live with my in-laws."

"What?" he asks, and I suddenly hear he is in his truck.

"Yeah, Lizzie came into the house pissed and stormed upstairs. He gave me this horse shit excuse about her not sleeping. Daisy is the one who said she wasn't going to live with them."

"Why would he ask that?" he asks the question that no one has the answer to.

"I have no clue, but you can bet your ass if he doesn't call me, I'm going to show up at his work tomorrow. I don't give a shit anymore." He doesn't say anything as I rant and rave about them. "Where are you going?"

"Hailey's," he says. "I'm almost there. I left right after shift."

"Are you excited?" I ask him, and he says yes. We talk for a bit more until he arrives.

I hang up the phone, and the doorbell rings. I walk to the door and open it. A man stands before me with a clipboard in one hand. "Samantha Schneider," he says, looking at the paper and then up at me again.

"Yes," I say with one hand holding the door. His hand reaches out with papers folded in his hand. My hand reaches out to get them.

"You've been served," he says and turns and walks away. I close the door as my hands shake, holding the letter.

I turn it over in my hand, unfolding the pages, and I don't even realize I've hit the floor when I do.

I see nothing except the names at the top corner of the plaintiffs—Judy and Adrian Schneider—and then my name under the defendant. And what I see under that stops my blood cold.

They are suing me for custody of the girls, deeming me unfit and alienating their affection.

The sob rips through me, and my hand moves to my chest. I run to grab my phone and call Elliot first, and he doesn't answer. "Please call me back," I say between sobs. "Please."

I then call Judy, and I'm sent straight to voicemail. "Judy, you need to call me back," I whisper as I sob.

I don't know what to do. I don't know who to call, so I call the only lawyer I know. When the secretary answers, I ask to speak to Mr. Feldman. I'm transferred right away, and he picks up. "Mr. Feldman, this is Samantha Schneider. I'm calling because I got served papers today from my in-laws."

"I'm aware," he says, not shocked at all. "I suggest you get yourself a lawyer." He then hangs up on me.

I look up in shock at the phone. What the hell am I going to do? I sit here, and for the first time in my life, I regret the day I fucking met Eric.

Opening the computer, I google family lawyers in the area. I call the first one my eyes land on and make an appointment for the next day. The whole day is spent with me reading and rereading the papers I was served. I hide them away before I get the girls and try to act as normally as I can. My phone beeps, showing me Elliot responded to my text.

I'm sorry.

It's the only thing he says, two words. He didn't even have the fucking balls to pick up the phone and call me. That night, I make the girls sleep with me, hugging both of them while they sleep, and I cry silently, kissing their heads.

I ignore the call from Blake and the texts. He has enough going on right now. The next day when I walk into the lawyer's office, he reads the paper and looks up at me. "It is very rare that the grandparents are awarded custody when one of the parents is still alive."

I fill him in on the whole double life that Eric led. He tells me what I don't really want to hear. "You need to find a character witness who can confirm all this," he tells me, and my shoulders slump. I leave the lawyer's office with a list of things I need to do and papers that need to be filled out. When the girls come home, I again try to pretend everything is normal, but Lizzie senses something.

I let them sleep in their own bed that night and then pick up the phone and dial the one person I know who can help me—Blake.

He answers after two rings, a little breathless. "Hey," he says, and I lose whatever I was holding in me, letting go of everything.

"Samantha," he says, "breathe for me, baby, just breathe."

I listen to his words as I try not to hyperventilate. "I need your help," I tell him quietly.

"Anything," he answers without hesitation.

"I need you to be a character witness," I tell him and wait for the next question I know is coming.

"For what?" he asks, and I say the words I dreaded all day long.

"My in-laws are suing me for custody of the girls," I say quietly and then cry. "They are going to take my babies away from me." He doesn't say anything else.

"I'm on my way," he says and disconnects, and I don't know why, but I suddenly feel like everything is going to be okay.

Chapter Twenty

Blake

One minute, I'm having pizza, and the next, I'm rushing back to my truck, kissing Hailey goodbye, and hightailing it to Samantha's house.

I had no idea that when I pulled up to Hailey's cottage on the beach, I would find such a different person. She was not even the old Hailey; she was a better Hailey. I thought I would have to snap her out of it, but she smiled and laughed and looked in love. Then I found out why when a soft knock came, and I found her in Jensen's arms.

I hated being the one to break her out of that when I gave her the letter. Actually, she didn't even fucking take the letter; she just left. Lucky for me, Jensen came and made her okay, brought her back to center. She took the letter to her room and then told me we were eating pizza for dinner.

I sat at the table with Hailey and Jensen, who showed up with his adorable daughter. Not only did my sister fall in love with Jensen, but she was also head over heels for Mila.

Crystal was also doing well and came in with Jensen's cousin, Gabe, who was also her boss. I couldn't put my finger on it, but there was more to that story, and I made a note to ask her about it when we got home.

Then my phone rang, and I went outside to take it. I had been calling Samantha for two days now with no answer, but her voice was unrecognizable. The hairs on my neck stood up right away. Then she asked me to be a character witness, and my mind was going around and around.

"My in-laws are suing me for custody of the girls," she said so quietly I was afraid I misunderstood her. "They are going to take my babies away from me." My blood ran cold and only one thing went through my mind was over my dead fucking body would someone take the girls away from her.

"I'm on my way," I say, disconnecting then telling Hailey there was an emergency. I didn't mention anything because I didn't have time to tell her about Samantha. I wasn't sure I wanted to share her yet.

I got in my car, thankful she is halfway between Hailey's home and my home. I pull up in her driveway around eleven. I don't even have to call her because she's standing at the door. Leaning against it, she watches as I put the truck in park, get out, and walk up the stairs to her. Taking her in my arms right away, I hold her while she cries. Quietly, I pick her up around her waist and bring her inside the house. "It's going to be okay," I tell her while I hold her. "Let me see what they sent you," I ask her, and she disengages herself from my arms and takes my hands to lead me up the stairs to her bedroom, then locks the door after I step inside. She goes to the dresser where she opens the drawer and takes out the paper.

She comes to me, and I sit on the edge of the bed as I read the papers. Those motherfuckers are really fucking suing her. "What did your lawyer say?" I ask, and the only thing that pops in my head is that I don't trust him. I don't trust anyone, but the one man I know would have my back, no questions asked. She sits next to me sideways, her legs crossed and leaning on mine.

"He said it's rare that grandparents are awarded custody if one of the parents is still alive." She swallows and looks at me; her beautiful face in so much pain, her brown eyes filled with tears, "I can't lose them." She shakes her head. "I won't."

My hand cups her face, my thumb catching a tear that runs down her face. "You won't lose them." I swallow and look down and then up again. "I need to tell you something."

She looks at me, hanging onto my every word, trusting me so fucking completely. "My father is the best family lawyer …" She shakes her head.

Getting off the bed, she says, "I can't do that," as she paces in front of me. "I can't ask him that." I reach out my hand and stop her, bringing her to me. She stands between my open legs, her hands resting on my shoulders. "I won't do that to him or to Hailey."

"You need the best," I tell her. "That's him."

"I don't know, Blake," she says softly. "It's already weird that we are talking, and all this," she says, looking down and then back up, our eyes meeting. "How did this happen?" she asks, and I don't know what she's asking.

It's a loaded question. My hands go to her hips. "Someone told me once that everything happens for a reason." I smile as she finally smiles just a bit. "Maybe it was fate."

She shrugs. "Do you think he would listen to my case?" she asks me.

"I think there is no reason we can't ask him," I tell her, and I notice not for the first time today it's a we—not a you, not a me, an us. "After you put the kids on the bus tomorrow, we can drive down and see my father."

"I want to change one of my answers," she tells me. "One

thing I would change is Eric being the father of my girls," she says, closing her eyes and shaking her head. The need to bring her on my lap is so strong my heart aches, and the need to put my hand on her face and drag her lips to mine makes my hands heavy, so heavy. Her eyes open, and I'm stuck here, my body almost as if made of stone.

I can't move, and I can't breathe; the only thing I can do is blink my eyes and take her in. The woman who was the cause of Hailey's hurt, the woman whose house we came to and demanded answers. The woman who slowly, ever so fucking slowly, got stronger and stronger, and even more gradually has made a home in my broken heart.

"I thought of taking the girls and moving," she says softly. "Get away from here. Somewhere no one knows us. Somewhere I don't feel out of place walking into a grocery store."

"What do you mean?" I ask her.

She looks down and then up again. "My in-laws know everyone, and ever since they stopped talking to me, it's just been weird. I'm afraid to meet them in public, so I don't make eye contact with anyone, and I have everything delivered just so I don't cross paths with them or anyone they know."

"You never told me that," I say and think about this house. No wonder she is changing everything; it's her fucking prison.

"I didn't want to talk about it," she says, "but, yeah."

"Let's tackle one thing at a time. Let's get your girls safe, and then we'll work on getting you out of here."

"You really think everything is going to be okay?" she asks me.

"No, I don't think; I know." I look at her and see the tiredness fall through her. "Why don't you go to sleep? I'll go sleep on the couch and leave before the kids get up, and we'll go see Dad after."

"You can just lie here; the door is locked, and if the girls wake, you can hide." She smiles and goes to her side of the bed. I look over my shoulder at her. "I got a new mattress," she whispers. "It's Eric free." I shake my head and laugh. I lie on the top of the covers while she gets under. She is softly snoring even before I get comfortable, and I lie awake for a long, long time as so many things race through my head, so many things that I need to say, so many things I need to finally come to peace with.

"Wake up, sunshine." I hear her voice, but I swear I think I'm dreaming. I open my eyes and see her on the bed on her knees. "The kids just got on the bus."

"I must have slept through it," I say, blinking as she turns to hand me a cup of coffee.

"I told them I just washed the carpet in the room and not to go in." She smiles. "I guess they bought it."

I smile, taking a sip of the hot coffee. "Carpet cleaning?"

She throws her head back and laughs. "Lame, right?"

She gets up, and I see she's already dressed. "Are you ready?" I ask her, and she nods. I get up, going to the bathroom, and then come out. "Let's go," I say, happy to get this all over with.

"Bring everything, even the picture of Hailey and him and his letter." She nods and grabs the letter and the picture. She looks down when we walk out of the house to my truck almost as if she's hiding herself. I fucking hate this; she should be walking proud, walking with her head held high.

The drive is quiet, and when we stop for gas, I call my father.

"Hello?" He answers on the second ring.

"Hey, Dad, are you at the office?" I ask him. Usually, he is there, but sometimes he works from home.

"I am. What's up?" he asks.

"I need your help," I tell him. "I'll be there in about an hour. Will you have time for me?"

"Yes," he says and doesn't bother asking questions. I disconnect when she walks out of the gas station with two waters in her hand. Her walk now is more sure, more comfortable than when she walked out of her house.

When we pull up to my father's office, I shut off the truck. I look over and see her hands shaking. "It's going to be okay." I grab one, and she just shakes her head and swallows. We walk in, and I smile at Beatrice.

"Look at this handsome fellow," she says, smiling at me. "Oh, and you brought a lady friend." I laugh; they are so old school.

"Hey, my dad is expecting me," I tell her and then look over at Samantha. "You ready?" I ask.

"No," she says, "I think I'm going to be sick." I can see she is shaking.

"Let's go." I grab her hand and walk to the back where his office is. I knock on the door, and he yells for me to come in.

I turn the handle and open the door, seeing him sitting behind his big oak desk with pictures of us all around the room. He takes his glasses off and stands up when he sees me with Samantha.

His eyes go to me and then her; the silent questions are about a mile a minute, and I give him a nod, telling him we will talk.

"Dad," I say when he looks at me again. "This is Samantha, a friend of mine."

He extends his hand to shake hers with a smile, walking around the desk. "Nice to meet you, Samantha," he says, and she smiles at him. "Please, come sit." He points at the sitting area away from his desk in the corner. Samantha sits on the loveseat, and I sit next to her. My father sits in the single chair. Looking at us, he asks, "What can I do to help?" I hand him the paper from the lawyer. He opens the letter, reading just the first couple of lines, and his eyes snap up.

"Dad, this is Samantha Schneider," I say, and his mouth opens.

Chapter Twenty-One
Samantha

I know right away when his head snaps up that he knows who I am. I sit next to Blake, trying to bask in his warmth, and I end up shaking.

"Dad, this is Samantha Schneider," he says, grabbing my little hand in his, and his father's mouth opens and closes.

"Blake," he says, turning to look at him.

"I know what you're thinking, Dad," he says, "but she needed the best, and you're the best."

He puts the papers down and then gets up and goes to his phone. "Beatrice, call Joanne and tell her to come in please."

Then he looks at me. "I'm sorry, but I can't keep this from my wife." And I smile and look at Blake, knowing right away that is where he got it from.

"I don't mind," I tell him and then look at Blake. "Killing two birds with one stone, right?" I push his shoulder, and he looks down and smiles.

"Would you like something to drink while we wait?" he asks while he looks at me. This man, whose daughter was broken and treated so unfairly by Eric's family, who were mine, is standing there offering me something to drink instead of telling me to take my things and fuck off. I shake my head. "Before your mother gets here, can you answer a couple of questions?" he asks me and Blake.

"What in the ever-loving fuck is going on?" He sits down, crossing his legs. "Blake?"

I laugh at him; such a gentleman and he throws out the F bomb. "I went to visit her with Crystal right before Hailey decided to leave. Then I called and checked on her, and we've been friends ever since." I know it shouldn't bother me that he said we've been friends, but my stomach burns. I smile at him and then look down, trying to hide my eyes. I hear women's voices and then the door opens and a beautiful woman walks in. Henry gets up to greet his wife who looks like she sped here.

"I got here as soon as I could," she says breathlessly to her husband and then turns to look at us, her eyes taking in that Blake still has my hand in his. "Blake," she says and then looks at me. I get up, putting out my hand.

"Mrs. Williams, my name is Samantha." She smiles as she takes my hand.

"Samantha, it's a pleasure to meet you," she says, and Henry finally tells her to sit down.

"So what is this meeting about?" she says as she sits in the chair where Henry was sitting. He now sits on the arm of the chair.

I look at Blake, and then I look at Henry. Both of them are unsure of how to start things, so I do what I need to do. I take a deep breath and squeeze Blake's hand.

"My name is Samantha Schneider," I say, and her eyes suddenly go big. "I was married to Eric," I start, and the tears spill over. "We have two girls. Two beautiful girls, beautiful girls," I say, and the tears don't stop, no matter how many times I blink them away. "I was a ward of the state and have no family. None. I was a crack baby," I tell them, and Blake lets my hand go. I look at him, expecting to see his judgment, but instead, he puts his arm around my shoulder, bringing me closer to him and kissing my forehead. I know I have to continue. "When I was nineteen, I met Eric and fell in love with him. His family became my family. They welcomed me with open arms." My hands now come together as I get nervous. "They were the family I always dreamed of. I finally had a mother and father who loved me, and two brothers who would do anything for me. A husband who gave me a family," I say, smiling through the tears. "But then he died, and his box of secrets came out. I didn't want to sit at the table while they put him on a throne."

I look down while I continue, "I couldn't do it, and then it was like I was shunned. They stopped calling, they stopped coming by"—I look up—"and suddenly, I was back to being alone, but this time, I had my girls." Blake's mother has tears running down her face as I'm talking, Henry's hand is holding her shoulder. "They didn't like the changes I was making. I repainted the house, and I was moving on. To them, I was trying to erase Eric from the home we shared." I reach forward and grab a Kleenex from the table. "How can I erase him from our lives when my girls have his eyes?" I say on a sob. "How can I erase him from my life when every single time I turn around, his memory is there?"

I don't know how I go on, but I do. "They said if I was woman enough, he wouldn't have done what he did. That if I was more supportive and less demanding, he would have stayed with me." I hear a hiss and expect it to be from Blake, but it's from Henry.

"Yesterday, they served me with court papers," I say, crying out now, the sobs too much to keep down. "They want my girls. I can't let them have my girls." I can't go on because I'm in

Blake's arms. My face is against his chest as he whispers to me that everything is going to be okay. I force myself to stop, force myself to face the music.

"Oh my God." I hear Blake's mother whisper. I look up at Blake and then turn around.

"I'm sorry, I shouldn't bring this to you. I know that my in-laws have done some despicable things to Hailey, and I just want you to know I had no idea."

"You poor, poor child," his mother says. "It almost killed Hailey, but she had us, and you had no one." She shakes her head and gets up. Coming to my side, she grabs my hand. "Henry, what can she do?" she asks her husband.

I look and see that Henry is reading the court papers. "I called another lawyer yesterday, and he thinks I have a shot, but I would need character witnesses to show the judge how Eric was. I have a letter he wrote me that I found when I was cleaning out his closet." Blake hands the paper to him, and he opens it and reads it. His hand squeezes the paper so tight that his knuckles turn white.

He gets up and calls Beatrice. "I need you to photocopy this, and I need you to call the lawyer and set up a phone meeting with him. See if he's available now," he says to her and then turns to look at me. "There is no fucking way those children will go to these people," he says, using the F word again.

"I need to use the bathroom," I whisper to Blake, who gets up and leads me to the washroom, where I wash off my face. Walking out, I see him leaning against the wall. "You didn't have to wait."

"I know"—he looks at me—"I wanted to."

He leads the way back to the office, and I hear Henry's voice rise. "You really think you have a leg to stand on?" His voice gets louder. "You're as delusional as your clients are," he says and then looks up. "See you in court." He hangs up. "So it seems that your in-laws are out for blood. Do you have a savings account with just your name?" he asks, and I nod my head. "Transfer everything to that one. Do it now." He looks at Blake. "I hope you know what you're doing, son, because this isn't good."

I swallow as I look at him. "What is going on?" I ask him, my heart racing.

"You need to transfer all your money now because if I know this type of lawyer, they are already freezing everything that you own with Eric."

"Fuck," Blake says, and I turn to look at him. "Come with me," he says. I follow him to Beatrice's desk, and he asks her to get up. "Do it now."

I log on and make all the transfers to the one account no one knows about because I just opened it. "Done," I say. He nods, and we walk back into the room. "All done."

"Is it just in your name?" he asks again.

"Yes, I just opened it when I went to the bank." I shrug. "No idea why."

"Okay, so I'm going to give it to you straight," he says, and I stand here with Blake on one side of me, and now his mother on the other. "We have a court appearance in two days. The court is going to assign a social worker to talk to the girls."

"But …" I shake my head, but I stop when I see him look at me.

"We need to get sworn statements from the kids' teachers. Was Eric present?" he asks me, and I look at him.

"He lived here half the time," I reply. "He didn't even know what grade they are in."

"Good, that will work. I'll call the school today," he says. "Now, I'm going to ask you some questions, and I want the truth. Don't sugar coat anything."

I nod at him. "Are you with anyone?"

"No," I say, but I look down. "Blake is my only friend."

"Are you on any type of drug?" he asks, and I almost step back. "If they test you, will you be clean?"

"Yes," I say to him. "I barely take Advil."

"Have you ever beaten the children, slapped them, sent them to bed without supper? Anything?"

"Dad," Blake hisses.

"Never," I say, and he nods. "I would never. I was a social worker before I got pregnant," I tell him.

"When can I meet the girls?" he asks, and I look at him. "I need to talk to them."

"Tonight," Blake says. "We can get them and make it in time for dinner, then we can drive back."

"Perfect," he says. "Now that all this is out of the way, I need to have some lunch." He looks at Mrs. Williams. "You going to take your husband to lunch?"

She looks at him like he hangs the moon and the stars. "You bet I will." She smiles, and Blake groans while I laugh and turn to block the sound in his arm.

Chapter Twenty-Two

Blake

We make it home with a couple of minutes to spare, and she runs in the house, grabbing their pjs and packing it. "They can fall asleep on the way back," she says. "I'm going to follow you, so you don't have to come back and then go home."

"Not a chance in hell are you driving back in the dark after what happened today," he says. "I'll be fine. I'm off all week, so I'll sleep tomorrow."

"What do we tell the girls?" She turns to ask me.

"The truth," I tell her. "I mean, not about Hailey and all that, but that her grandparents want to take them away from you. They might not get it, but don't let them scare you."

She nods her head and then walks out of the house, going to the bus. She walks in a couple of minutes later with the cutest kids ever. They sure do have Eric's eyes, but that's it; they are just as gorgeous as their mom.

"Girls," she says, "this is my friend Blake." The girls look at me; Daisy almost hides her face with Lizzie standing beside her mother. "His family invited us over for dinner, isn't that fun?"

I squat down so I'm eye level with Daisy. "It's so nice to meet you guys. Your mom has told me all about you," I say, and Daisy finally smiles. "We should get going; I live a little far," I say, getting up. "Is it okay if we take my truck, or did you guys want to take your mom's?" I ask Lizzie to have her make the decision.

"Can we take Mom's?" she asks unsure.

"Yup. I've always wanted to drive a mini-van," I say, smiling, and Lizzie even laughs.

"We can watch movies in Mommy's car," Daisy says as we walk out of the house. I watch as Lizzie gets in, and Samantha helps Daisy in.

Halfway there, she turns around and looks in the back of the car. "Okay, girls," she starts, and they both look at her. "Grandma and Grandpa want you to go live with them," she says. Lizzie bursts out crying, and she reaches in the back to hold Lizzie's hand. "But I am going to fight them to make sure you stay with me."

"I don't want to go," Daisy now starts. "I want to stay with you, Mommy."

"I know you do, honey, which is why we are going to meet Blake's dad. He's going to help me fight to keep you."

"Okay," Lizzie says.

"He's going to want to talk to you and ask you questions, and you have to be honest with him, okay?" She looks at me as they both say yes. She turns around and looks out the window, a tear coming down.

"I never want to see them again," Lizzie says quietly. "I'm never going there."

"Me too," Daisy says, copying her sister. I look at Samantha, who closes her eyes, putting her hand in front of her mouth to stop the sob. I reach over, grabbing her hand. We pull up to my parents' house, and I see Nanny's car right away. I knew my mother wouldn't let this opportunity pass.

"Ready?" I ask as I shut off the car. Looking back, I see the girls nodding and getting out. I round the car and see that Samantha is carrying Daisy with Lizzie holding her hand. I walk to them, and Lizzie grabs my hand. All of us are connected. "It's going to be okay, Lizzie," I tell her, and she just nods.

We walk into the house, and the smell of roast fills the air. That and apple pie. I hear the hustle coming from the kitchen and walk with them. "I'm here," I say, and my mother turns around and takes in me holding hands with Lizzie.

"Oh my God," she whispers as she blinks tears away. She takes off her apron and comes to us. "You are so beautiful," she says to Lizzie who smiles at her. "My name is Joanne," she tells them as she looks at Daisy, "and you. I've never seen a more beautiful five-year-old."

"I'm almost six," she says, and my mother laughs. My father comes to her side.

"Hello, girls, I'm so happy you could come and have dinner with us," he says, holding my mother's shoulder like he always does.

"Are you going to be the one who is going to fight for Mommy?" Lizzie is the first to ask, and my mother has to look down, and I know why because the tear falls. "I want to stay with my mommy."

"I'm going to do everything I can to make it happen. I promise," he says, and then I hear Nanny in the background from somewhere in the house.

"If that doesn't happen, we can go underground." Samantha looks shocked and laughs as my grandmother comes in the room with tears in her eyes as she spots me with Samantha. "My name is Nanny," she says to Samantha. "It's a pleasure to meet you. And your beautiful girls." She looks at them and then at me. "Look at you. I never thought I would live to see the day."

She turns around. "Who is going to help me set the table?" she asks, and Daisy squirms out of Samantha's arms.

"I do the forks at home. But not the knives. It's dangerous," she says, following Nanny. "Lizzie does the glasses," she informs Nanny, but Lizzie doesn't leave the kitchen as she looks at my father.

"Mommy said you need to ask me questions," she says, and he nods at her. "Can we do it now?"

"Yes," my father says and walks to the study that he converted into an office. I follow him with Lizzie and Samantha.

"Is it okay that your mom and Blake stay in the room, or would you like them to go?" he asks her, grabbing a yellow legal pad.

"They can stay," she says, and my father points at the big couch he has against the wall. Samantha sits with Lizzie next to her and me on the other side of Lizzie. "I know who you are," she tells us quietly, looking down and then looking up.

"You're Hailey's brother." I sit here shocked, but not more shocked than Samantha, whose mouth is hanging open.

"I heard Uncle Ethan and Elliot talk in the garage about Hailey's brother, Blake." She looks down at her hands. "Are you still going to make sure I stay with Mommy even if Daddy hurt Hailey?" she asks my father the question.

"Yes," he says right away. "You didn't do that, and your mom didn't do that. But your dad did. It's no one's fault but his."

"Okay," she says, and then he starts asking her questions. She answers them perfectly.

"Can I go see if I can set the table?" She turns to Samantha, and I answer for her.

"Yes. If not, I'm sure my mom will give you something to do."

We wait for the door to close, and then Samantha looks at

us. "I had no idea she would piece it together. I knew she heard them, but …"

"Doesn't matter," my father says, getting up. "I meant what I told her. This isn't on you; it's on Eric. Your daughter loves you, and from what she told me, you're a great mom."

"Thank you." He nods and walks out. "I don't think I can ever thank him enough." She looks at me. "Or you." She smiles and looks down.

"It's nothing," I tell her, and it's the truth. We would do it for anyone, but she isn't nobody. She's somebody.

"Come and eat!" I hear my mother yell, so I get up and hold my hand out to her. Dinner goes off without a hitch, my father taking the chance to ask Daisy questions without her knowing.

When everyone is finally finished, we look at the clock and see it's already past eight. "We should get going. By the time we get home, it's going to be past eleven," she says from beside me.

She thanks my mother for the meal and is a little bit shocked when she hugs her. The girls are all giggly when Nanny tells them the next time, she is going to take them for ice cream.

The kids change right before we leave and are asleep within thirty minutes from leaving my parents. "I think I'm going to sleep for a whole week when this is over," she says. Leaning her head on the window, she too falls asleep. I pull up to the house, just after ten forty-five, and look over at her. She is softly snoring. I take my finger and rub her cheek softly; she is so beautiful and strong. "You're home," I say when she blinks her eyes open. "Go open the door, and I'll bring the girls in," I tell her, and she opens the door as I carry in first Daisy and then Lizzie.

"Do you want a coffee before you go?" she asks, yawning.

"No. I'm going to go so you can get some sleep," I tell her as she walks me to the door. She reaches up on her tippy toes and hugs me.

Her arms go around my neck as she whispers, "Thank you for everything." I just nod.

"Lock up," I tell her, walking to my truck. She waits for me to drive away before going inside. Thirty minutes later, the phone rings. "What are you still doing up?" I ask her.

"I couldn't fall asleep knowing you were driving," she says softly into the phone. "So it's just easier if we talk till you get home."

I laugh, and she asks about Nanny, and how crazy she is. I tell her the story of her husband dying and leaving her a widow with three children and debt. I don't even see the time fly by, and I'm suddenly pulling up into my driveway a little after eleven thirty. "I'm home," I tell her.

"Okay," she says, and she asks me the question she usually does. "What would you change if you could?"

I don't stop, nor do I have to think twice about it. "I would have kissed you tonight before I left." I don't wait for her to disconnect; this time, it's me who does it.

I walk into the house and am locking the door when my phone beeps. I know it's from her; I'm just not sure I want to know what she says, but I stop when I read it.

I would have let you.

Chapter Twenty-Three

Samantha

I pull on the blue pants, shimmying myself into them. I still haven't gained much weight back, so they are a little loose. I pair it with a white silk button-up shirt that has vertical blue stripes. Today is our first appearance in front of the judge, and I barely slept a wink last night.

I grab my blue high heels and walk downstairs, opting to leave my hair down. The doorbell rings, and I open the front door to see Blake and his parents. "Come in," I say, smiling at them, surprised that his mother came.

We haven't discussed what he said, nor have we discussed my text I sent him after. "I didn't know that you were coming, Mrs. Williams." I look at her.

"Call me Joanne," she says, "Oh, of course, I would come."

"We really should go, so we aren't late," Henry says to me as I turn, grabbing my heels and purse. "Let's take my car and arrive together, so they don't get you without me."

I walk down the steps to the car and sit in the back with Blake. He reaches out to hold my hand. "Thank God tomorrow is Saturday," I tell him, thankful I'll be able to sleep in. He just looks out the window and nods. Maybe he didn't mean it; maybe it was in the moment and now the moment has passed.

My stomach starts swirling when we pull up in the parking lot. I see Ethan's truck is there. "I think I'm going to be sick," I say out loud when I didn't mean to.

"You got this," Blake says, and I wish I had as much faith in me as he did.

I walk up the steps to the courthouse with Henry next to me, followed by Blake and his mother. We walk in, and Henry walks to courtroom number two. I'm looking down when he stops, and I see why he stopped. In front of the courtroom door stands the Schneiders.

I look at them as my mother-in-law just looks past me, and my father-in-law looks at me with a sneer. Ethan and Elliot don't even bother making eye contact with me but look straight into Blake's eyes.

Henry doesn't even bother giving them the time of day. He opens the door and smiles at me. "Shall we?" he says, and I nod at him.

"How?" I hear Joanne behind me, and I turn to look at her. "How can they treat family like that?"

"Easy," I say. "I'm not their family." I've come to terms with it.

"Let's go sit down," Henry says as we sit down at the table on the left-hand side. The door opens, and the Schneiders walk in with their lawyer. Judy and Adrian sit down next to each other at the table to the right. The lawyer walks over to our table, extending his hand, and Henry takes it.

"I've been instructed to offer you fifty thousand dollars for the girls. All she has to do is sign and it can be over." My skin goes cold, but I'm not the only one. Henry looks at him and leans back in his chair.

"I'd really hate to see you lose in court, so how about they drop this shit and keep their fifty thousand dollars. In the end, they can probably have a relationship with the girls."

"Not going to happen," he says.

"I was hoping you'd say that." He smiles. "Did you get the amended copy of the court papers?"

"No. What are you talking about?" He looks at him as Henry laughs again.

"My bad." He leans over, opening his briefcase. "I filed this late last night. You should be getting a copy sometime today, but I'll clarify it with the judge." Henry hands him the paper; he snatches it and looks back at Henry.

"You've got to be fucking kidding me."

"Nope," he says, looking at me. "I'm taking this very personal, so I'm coming out swinging," he says, and the lawyer walks away.

I lean over and whisper, "What is going on?"

"You'll see." I look over, and the lawyer doesn't have time to tell the Schneiders because the bailiff informs us to all rise.

The bailiff tells her, "This is the case of Schneider versus Schneider."

"Thank you, Todd," she tells him.

I look over at the judge. "Good morning, my name is Judge Kirk, and I will be the one presiding over this case." She looks over at us and then opens the file. "Oh, this is interesting. We have a countersuit." I sit here, looking straight ahead, not showing that I have no idea what all this means. "Mr. and Mrs. Schneider, you're suing Mrs. Schneider for custody of your grandchildren, Lizzie and Daisy Schneider."

Their lawyer gets up and says, "Yes, your honor, we have reason to believe she is unfit and is alienating their affections from them."

I force myself not to roll my eyes. The judge nods to him, and he sits down. "Mrs. Schneider, you are suing the Schneiders for a hundred thousand dollars for the emotional distress of Lizzie and Daisy Schneider."

I look at Henry, who gets up and answers. "Yes, your honor. The children have just lost one parent and informing them that they might lose another was traumatic, to say the very least."

She nods. "The court is appointing a social worker to visit the children." She looks down and reads a paper, then looks up at my in-laws. "I really hope that you know what you're doing," she warns them. "They just lost a parent. I would hate for them to lose someone else they love just for spite. We reconvene in two weeks." She gets up, and we stand, waiting for her to walk out of the courtroom. My head falls right away, and I look over at Henry.

"Oh, by the way, you're countersuing them," he says, and I laugh quietly, turning and walking out with him. Elliot comes up to us.

"Sam," he says, "I'd like to come and see the girls."

"No," I say right away, and I think I shock him, but I don't stop. "I trusted you to take care of them, to take them camping, and what did you do? Do you know Lizzie cried the rest of the afternoon?" I tell him, and he looks shocked. "Do you know every single day Daisy asks me if you're going to take them away?"

"Sam …"

"No," I snap and advance on him, but Henry gets in front of me. "I called you and begged you to call me back, but you didn't even have the gall to call me back, knowing that I was going to be served. You stayed in my house, and you ate at my table. You know damn well I'm a good mom."

"I'm sorry," he says softly.

"Yeah, that's all I get from you lately," I say and turn around, looking for Blake. I see him right at my back, and I feel good. I feel safe. I feel that it's going to be okay.

"Mrs. Williams, I would love to have you over for lunch, but I have to be honest, I suck at cooking," I tell her as she laughs.

"That's okay, honey, how about we hit a restaurant?" she asks, grabbing her husband's hand and walking out, leaving me and Blake alone.

He looks around and then comes closer to me, whispering, "How opposed are you if the first time I kissed you was in front of my parents?"

I look at him. "Um … very."

"Right, so I suggest we speed up lunch," he says, and my mouth becomes dry. "Shall we?" He ushers me out, but the only thing on my mind is his lips touching mine.

Chapter Twenty-Four

Blake

I watch her walk to the car with her head down and her shoulders slouched. When my mother chose the deli next to her house, she sat in the corner booth almost sinking to the floor. We all saw it, and I wasn't the only one who hated it.

"Starting next week, I'm going to make a list of people we can call to the stand on your behalf," my father says once we get to her house.

"The list won't be long," she says quietly. "I think I have Blake and the kids' teacher, but …" She shrugs her shoulders.

It's the dreaded time for us to leave, and I haven't kissed her yet. I've done nothing but think about kissing her. I've played the scene over and over in my head.

"What are you guys doing this weekend?" I ask her, stopping the conversation about the trial.

"I have no idea," she says, looking at me confused.

"Why don't you and the kids come and spend the weekend with us?" I smile while she tries to swallow. "The city fair is in town, and we could take them to the zoo. Get their mind off all this."

"But where would we stay?" she asks, and I don't even wait for her to finish.

"With me," I say, and she opens her mouth. "I have two spare rooms." I see the wheels turning in her mind. "Why don't you ask the kids and see what they say?"

"That sounds like a great idea," my mother says. "Get them out of the house so they don't have to think about everything going on."

She looks around the table. "I guess I can ask them. It would be like a mini vacation." She gets up. "The bus should be here any second."

She walks out of the house while we sit at the kitchen table, and I look up. "I really hope you know what you're doing," my father says first.

"You need to tell Hailey," my mother whispers. "She needs to know what's going on."

"Mom, nothing is going on," I say, but even I don't believe my words.

"If nothing is going on, then why are we here?" my father asks.

"Well," I say, throwing my hands up. "Come on, we have to help her." My parents share a look.

"Yes, but we don't have to bring them home. We don't have to make sure she isn't going to break. We don't have to drive six hours in one day to make sure she and the girls are okay."

I roll my eyes. "Son, you are so invested and involved, you don't even see it."

"Dad."

"Do you know that when her brother-in-law came to talk to her, you gritted your teeth and flexed your hands every ten seconds?"

"They treat her like shit," I counter.

"When she sat in the restaurant and wanted the booth to swallow her whole, your leg shook the whole time," he continues.

"She's fucking embarrassed, and she has no reason to be."

"You invited her in your home to stay with you," he finally says, hitting the nail on the head. "You haven't dated one girl in seven years."

"It's too …"

"Oh, please," my mother says, finally rolling her eyes. "I finally see the look in your eye I thought would never be there. The light." She shakes her head. "There is nothing wrong with this. But"—she looks at my dad—"you would never do anything to hurt Hailey, anything, even start a friendship with a woman who holds a piece of her sadness."

"It's not her fau—" I say as my mother holds her hand up, turning to my father.

"What is this when I have no other questions and I'm done talking? Sort of like mic drop." She motions with her hand. I don't answer because the door opens, and Daisy comes running in first.

"We are going on a bacation," she says, and I laugh as she points at me. "At your house."

I smile at her. "Is that so?" I ask and look over to see Samantha and Lizzie come in, holding hands.

"So the girls think that spending the weekend away would great," she says, smiling. "Mr. and Mrs. Williams, if you want, you can go, and I can bring Blake back."

"That sounds great," my mother says and gets up, looking at the girls. "I'm going to get Henry to put our tent in the backyard, and maybe you guys can have a sleepover."

I look at my mom, not sure what she is getting at, but the kids get excited. "Can we do s'mores?" Lizzie asks. "And hot dogs on a stick?"

"Well, it isn't backyard camping without it," my father says as he pats their head. I watch the girls run upstairs to pack.

"I'm going to make sure that they don't over pack," she says, walking upstairs while I walk my parents out.

When I go back inside, I see the girls coming down with two backpacks. "We each have our own bag," Lizzie tells us, and I see that Samantha is coming down, and she has changed to jeans, carrying her own bag.

"Are we ready to go?" I ask her as she grabs a jacket and makes sure everything is off. "I'll load the girls."

We walk out, and the girls get situated. Samantha comes down the steps, getting into the passenger side, and we take off.

We make it home just in time for dinner, and my mother calls to tell us that she is coming over with pizza. I walk into the house, leading the girls to the spare bedroom. It has a queen-size bed, so they are all excited about sharing.

They dump their bags, and I look at Samantha. "Follow me," I tell her and go to the second guest room right next to mine. I open the door for her to see the queen-size bed, the white covers look super fluffy. "This is your room," I tell her and take her bag. She walks into the room and stands in the middle of the room while I dump the bag on the bed.

"This is perfect," she says, looking around. I walk to stand in front of her. "I don't know how to thank you," she starts saying and looks down, her hair falling in front of her face. I reach out to move her hair, and she looks up, smiling at me. My thumb rubs her cheek as I get closer to her. "Blake …"

"I haven't kissed a girl in seven years," I whisper to her as my head slowly moves down to hers, and she leans up, her breath hitching. I'm so close, close to finally tasting her when the door flies open, and Daisy yells, causing us to jump apart. "Pizza is here," she says and turns around.

"Well. That wasn't at all what I thought the first time would be like," I say and hear Samantha laughing.

"It'll be better when they are in bed." She grabs my hand, walking to the kitchen where my parents have the pizza set up on the counter, and my mother is making plates for the girls. It's the longest dinner of my life. I swear it lasted more than humanly possible for us to eat pizza.

Finally, my parents leave but not without promising to be back for breakfast and come with us to the zoo. When she leaves to put the kids in bed, I sit on the couch, my feet outstretched in front of me as I flip through the channels while I wait for her.

I hear the door close as she comes into the living room, her feet now bare. She comes to the couch, sitting on her legs next to me. "Hey," she says, looking at the television.

"Hey," I say, looking at her. "Was everything okay?"

"Yes." She smiles. "I couldn't think of a better night."

"I didn't think my parents would ever leave. Honest to God, they stayed forever."

She leans forward, laughing. "It wasn't that long," she says. My head turns to her.

She leans in and kisses my lips, just like that, no waiting, no talking, she just comes and places her lips on mine softly. My hand goes to her cheek, right as her mouth opens and her tongue slides against mine. She changes the angle to deepen the kiss, and it goes from soft to hungry. I grab her hips, bringing her to straddle me, and her knees land on either side of my hips. My hands get buried in her hair while her hands rub up my chest. When she gets to my neck, her hands thread through the hair at the base of my neck. I move her head from right to left as our lips stay together.

Neither of us wanting it to stop, we both try to lead the kiss. I finally let her lips go as our chests rise and fall at the same time.

"That was," she says softly, "perfect." She brings her lips down to mine again; this time, just giving me soft kisses.

"Your lips," I tell her, "were made for me to kiss." She comes back for another kiss. I kiss her until we are both breathless. I kiss her until I can't keep my eyes open any longer. I tuck her into bed, the kiss bringing me on the bed with her, and I fall asleep with her head tucked into my neck and my arms around her. And I feel suddenly at peace.

Chapter Twenty-Five

Samantha

This is the most comfortable bed I've ever slept in, ever. It's almost like it's a huge marshmallow. "Mommy. Blake made breakfast." I hear Lizzie say from the side of the bed, and my eyes open.

Blake. I smile. For the seven years he hasn't kissed, he's certainly made up for lost time. The minute I sat on that couch, I couldn't wait any longer and just went for it. I stretch my hands over my head and look at Lizzie. "Morning, baby." I smile at her. "What time is it?"

"Almost nine thirty," she says, and I jump out of bed. "Blake let us help make pancakes," she says when we walk out of the room. I walk into the kitchen and see that the table has been set.

"Morning," I say softly, going over to Daisy and kissing her nose. "Did you sleep okay?" I ask her, walking to the kitchen and Blake. I lean up and kiss his lips, and then we both stop, forgetting that the kids are here. We both look over and see that Lizzie saw but then smiled and looked down, sitting down. "Morning," I whisper to him. Taking him in, track pants and t-shirt, his hair all out of place from sleep or from my hands.

"Your coffee is on the counter." He points with the spatula in his hand while he flips the pancake.

"I can't believe I slept so late," I tell him, picking up my cup and taking a sip.

"Yeah, I snuck out before the girls woke up, and by the time I got out of the shower, Daisy walked out and asked if she could have pancakes."

I put the cup down and look at this man. Two months ago, I didn't even know him, yet I couldn't picture my day without him now. A man who I hated, a man who slowly fixed my broken pieces.

"What's wrong?" he asks, coming to me after he puts the last pancake on the plate.

"Nothing," I say, shaking my head. "Just thinking."

"We—" He doesn't have time to say anything because the doorbell rings, and then the front door opens.

"I heard that my special two girls are in town." We hear Nanny from the front room as she walks toward the kitchen. She sees the girls and claps her hands together. "There they are. I heard you were here, and I couldn't stay away," she says, going over to them and kissing their head. "Good morning, you two."

"Good morning," I say. "Would you like some coffee?"

"Oh, no," she says, then sits at the table. "I heard you're going to the zoo and then backyard camping." She turns to look at the kids. "Joanne was taking the sleeping bags out when I dropped by there. She is so excited," she says. The kids start talking, and they basically don't stop the whole time we eat. I sit at the table, and it just feels right. Everyone helps clear the table and get ready to go to the zoo.

It's hands down the best day. So easy and smooth, at one point, Blake carried Daisy on his shoulders when she complained she couldn't walk another step. Henry and Joanne were pointing out all the new things to the girls, who hung on their every word. Nanny even entertained animal sounds as we walked along the path.

We all went back to Joanne's house, and she dragged the kids into the backyard. I don't know who was more excited about the tent—Joanne or the kids. Henry built a little fire right outside, and she got the sticks and hot dogs so everyone could cook their own hot dogs. I don't think I've ever laughed so much in my life; my cheeks literally hurt from smiling.

My girls were at ease, and I was at ease. I walked the whole day without looking over my shoulder and without the fear I would run into someone who knew my in-laws or would want to see how I'm doing without Eric. Who would tell me what a great man he was and blah, blah, blah. I look over and see Daisy yawning.

"We should get going," I tell Blake, who gets up. The girls say goodbye to Joanne and Henry, giving them each a hug.

We walk into the house, and I tell them it's bath time. When the kids finish, I tuck them in, and they both fall asleep right away.

I walk out to the living room to find Blake, but it's empty, as well as the kitchen. I walk toward the back, calling his name. "Blake," I say. Walking into his room, I hear the shower running. The room is neat; a sitting chair in the corner with his clothes piled on it. I look around the bedroom, seeing that the bed is a king covered with a soft blue duvet and gray throw pillows. My eyes land on the picture of him and Frankie right next to his bed.

My feet move without my consent, my hand reaching out and grabbing the picture to look at them. Their smiles fill the picture. My finger moves over Blake's face; he looks so young and so happy. His green eyes bright and shiny.

Then my eyes go to a smiling Frankie, her wild curly black

hair blowing in what probably was a windy day. "Hey." I hear him say when he walks into the room, holding a towel around his hips.

"I'm sorry," I say, putting down the picture on the bedside table. "I shouldn't have come in here without …"

He walks to me, bending his head down. My eyes land on a lone wet drop on his chest, and it hypnotizes me. I didn't even realize he wasn't wearing a shirt, showing me that he is all muscle. His abs defined, his chest broad, and his arms full. "It's okay, Samantha," he says softly, and my eyes snap up to his eyes.

"She's beautiful," I say softly

"She really was," he says softly, coming closer to me, his scent hitting me right away. The need to run my hands up his chest, to pull him close, and kiss him is so big my heart beats so hard and loud.

"You look so happy," I say to him when we stand toe-to-toe.

"I was happy," he says, his hands moving to my hips. "Never thought I could be that happy again." He pulls me closer. "I was wrong." It's the last thing he says before he leans down or I lean up; either way, our lips touch. His hands move from my hips to my back, pulling me closer to him as my hands move around his neck. We both moan when I feel his hardness against my stomach. His lips leave me wanting more as he kisses my jaw, under my jaw, my neck. "Will you stay with me tonight?" he asks, and my body goes tense for a second. "Not for that," he says, laughing; the heat of his breath on my neck making me shiver. "Today was the first day in seven years I felt carefree." He kisses me softly. "The first time in seven years I didn't for one minute say why me." His kisses are even softer. "The first time my chest didn't feel like someone was sitting on it."

"Today, I walked without the weight on my shoulders," I tell him, and his head comes back while he looks in my eyes.

"Today, I walked that whole park without a worry in the world because I knew if anything happened, you were right there." I smile and lean forward to kiss his chest, right in the middle. My lips feel the pounding of his heart. "Today, I saw my girls smile, and laugh, and giggle, and be happy." His green eyes get teary. "Today, I saw them not have guilt over being happy. Today, I saw Lizzie, who has been quiet and observant the whole time, throw her head back and laugh." Now the tears come to my eyes. "Today, you gave that to them."

"Okay, so you're definitely staying in this room," he says, laughing, "but I have to change." He looks down at his towel and the tent under it. "Do you need to shower?" he asks me, and I nod. "Go get your things to shower in here, and I'll go check on the girls and leave their door open in case they call out."

I'm not used to sharing my responsibility with anyone or counting on anyone; it's just been me. "Okay," I say, going to my room and grabbing my things to head into his bathroom. The glass shower doors still have drops of water on them. I undress, setting the water, and walk under the rain shower. It's so perfect and relaxing; I throw my head back as the water flows through my hair. I open my eyes, taking in the charcoal gray shower tiles that match the wood wall. Such a man cave yet so homey. I grab his soap, open it up, and squeeze it a bit to smell him. I pour a little in my hand, rubbing my hands together and washing myself with it. I use my own shampoo, rinsing it through. Grabbing a towel to dry off, I wrap my wet hair and get dressed. I brush out my hair, braiding it on one side.

Opening the door, I see him already in bed with the television playing. I walk to the chair and set my clothes on top of his. Walking to the bed, I throw the covers over and get under the sheet, my heart hammering away. I get closer and closer to him, looking up and smiling. He leans down and kisses me. "You smell like me," he says, and I think I turn a shade of beet red. "I like it," he says before scooting down and facing me, his hand on my hip, our chests together. I lean forward, kissing the crook of his neck.

Humming, I lay my head on his shoulder, and his arms wrap around me. I take in his heat, his body, just him. I close my eyes for one minute, just to rest, and it's a second too long because I fall fast asleep. With his arms around me, I sleep like I'm floating on a cloud. We wake during the night, reaching for each other, and I kiss him each time I wake up and then fall back to sleep the minute his arms are around me. "Mommy." I hear my name softly from the side of the bed. "Mommy." I open my eyes to see Daisy. I get up and look over at Blake who is now awake and sitting up, looking over at me and then at Daisy. "I had a bad dream," she says, crawling into bed with me. "A monkey was coming after me to eat my candy," she says, and I laugh at her. She buries her head into my neck, and I wrap my arms around her. Blake settles behind me with his arms around me and Daisy.

He kisses the back of my neck softly. "Sleep," he says, and I do, till I hear my name again. "Mommy." I open my eyes and see Lizzie. "I don't want to sleep alone," she says, and I'm about to get up and go into the other room when Blake pushes to the edge of the bed, taking me with him. I bring Daisy with me, leaving Lizzie enough space to crawl into bed. "Did you fall asleep in here watching television?" Lizzie asks, looking at me.

"Yeah, she did," Blake says from behind me. "I didn't want to wake her."

I look at Lizzie looking at me and then Blake. "Okay," she says, closing her eyes and drifting off to sleep. Morning comes way too quickly, and I'm expecting to get up with some stiffness since we slept four in a bed, but it's the opposite. I wake up perfect, and we all get up at the same time.

The kids lie on the couch while we work side by side making breakfast. "What time do you work today?" I ask him, dreading that I have to go back home.

"I start at three," he says. "I leave at two thirty, but you can stay later if you want." He hands me a plate of toast.

"No, I'm going to head back to get the kids settled before school."

"Is it weird that I miss you?" he says, standing next to me.

"Only if it's weird that I miss you too," I say, buttering the toast. I dread sitting down and eating, and I dread the time flying by. I dread going around the house, making sure we don't forget anything. I dread fixing the beds and packing our stuff.

He brings the bags to the car while we follow him. "Blake, can we come back?" Daisy asks, stepping into the car.

"Anytime," he says, smiling and bending to kiss her cheek. "Get into your seat," he instructs, closing the door.

"I had so much fun," Lizzie says. "I want to come back soon," she says, and he bends and kisses her cheek also.

"I'll make it happen, Lizzie," he tells her with a wink while she gets into her side of the car. He pulls me by my hand to the back of the car. "I know they can still see us," he says, "but I can't not kiss you." He grabs my face in his hands and bends to kiss me. Softly, then a little more, until he's peeling himself away from me. "I'll see you Thursday," he says.

"What?" I ask him.

"Samantha, I'm off shift on Wednesday afternoon. So Thursday, I'm coming to see you and the girls." I don't think he's asking me, more like informing me.

"Okay," I say, walking with him hand in hand to the driver's side door. He opens the door, waiting for me to get in.

"Drive safe," he says. "Call me when you arrive." He leans in once more, kissing my cheek. "See you guys Thursday." He closes the door.

I pull away, looking at him in the rearview mirror. The thought of going back home fills me with sadness and anxiety. The girls watch a movie, leaving me with my own thoughts.

Chapter Twenty-Six

Blake

As I walk into the house four days later, the house feels almost dead. I walk by the room that the kids slept in, and all of a sudden, I think of changing it to maybe add a television, so the girls can watch it in here if they want.

The last four days have been tough, and Samantha is on edge again. Being at home, she is going back into her shell. Just yesterday, she got groceries from Amazon so she wouldn't have to see the delivery guy for fear that they would tell her in-laws. We speak every single night, and they even FaceTime me right before dinner.

I dump my bag on the bed, looking over at Frankie's picture. I kick off my shoes when my phone rings. "Hey, Dad," I say, answering right away.

"Hey, son, are you still on duty?" he asks me, and I sit on the bed.

"No, just got home," I tell him. "I'm going to sleep for a bit. What's up?"

"Can you come over for dinner tonight? We need to talk," he says, and I know something is wrong.

"What's the matter?" I say right away. "What happened?"

"Nothing yet, but I think we need to talk about some things," he says, and I nod even though he can't see me.

"Okay, I'll be over for dinner," I tell him.

The next person I call is Samantha, who answers after one ring. "Hey, you," she says softly.

"What are you doing?" I ask her.

"I'm painting my bedroom today."

"Really? What color?" I ask her, wondering what else she googled.

"Earthy brown," she says, laughing. "According to the internet," she starts, "it's the most relaxing color to have in the bedroom."

"Is that so?" I say, and she laughs again.

"Go to sleep," she says, "and call me later." After she hangs up, I grab the pillow she used when she slept in my bed, and her smell helps me fall asleep.

When I pull up to my parents' house, the front door is unlocked. "I'm here," I say loudly, walking into the kitchen while my mother pulls out a pot roast. "That smells so good," I tell her, kissing her cheek. "Where is Dad?"

"He's coming," she says, and he walks into the kitchen right then. I see him look at me and then my mother. I wait for us to sit before I ask the loaded question.

"What's the matter?"

He looks at my mother and then at me. "The Schneiders are going to be putting Samantha's house up for sale after the trial."

"What?" I say, my heart speeding up.

"I got a call from the lawyer this morning; it seems they own the house. Eric got it as a wedding gift. But they are going to gift it to their other son."

"They can't just do that?" I say, pushing away from the table, not even hungry anymore. "What about the girls?"

"They feel they'll get custody of them, so they don't want Samantha staying in their house. So …"

"Does she know?" I ask, and my father nods his head. "I told her this afternoon."

"What did she say?" I ask him, worried now how she must be doing.

"She actually laughed and said that she would give them whatever they wanted as long as she got the girls." He looks down and then up again. "She wants me to sue them for payment." My eyebrows pull together. "She figures she's maintaining the house, like a janitor, so she wants back pay. Oh, and money for her paint."

I throw my head back and laugh. "Well, I can't say she's cowering in the corner."

"Son," he says softly, "they have a shit load of witnesses." He looks at my mother. "They have many willing to sit on the stand and tell everyone she tricked him into marriage, getting pregnant without his consent."

"Oh, please"—I roll my eyes—"how can she force him to make her pregnant?"

"I know, I know." He holds up his hand. "But she has two people on her list."

"Well, then we gotta make fucking sure that we bury Eric even deeper than they have him."

"Son"—he looks at me—"you know they are going to try to paint you into a corner." He looks down and then up. "Especially now."

"Especially now what?" I ask.

"Son, she spent the weekend at your house."

"I'm her friend," I tell him, and my mother laughs, rolling her eyes.

"So she slept where?"

"In the spare bedroom," I tell them, and I'm not lying.

"Alone?" she asks, and I close my mouth. "Exactly."

"I don't think we should put you on the stand," he tells me. "We can put your mother instead."

"There is no way Samantha is going to be okay with that," I tell them.

"You're right," my father said. "She shot it down and took your name out of it also."

"What?" I whisper, looking at him.

"She said there was no way you were going to be painted as the bad guy; she didn't give a shit," he said. "Her words, not mine. She has the letter Eric left plus the letters from the teachers. I think her case is strong."

"Dad, she can't lose those girls," I tell him; my heart hurts with even the possibility that it might happen.

"The social worker is going to talk to Lizzie tomorrow, and then Daisy the day after," he tells me. "The court date is scheduled for next Friday," he says. "I take it you're coming?"

"Yeah," I say and then look at them. "I think I'm going to go." I look at my mother who only nods her head.

"Drive safely."

"Son, these people. I wouldn't put it past them to have someone following her and tracking her."

My head snaps up. "It's not going to look good in court if you spend the night."

I run my hands through my hair. "Fuck." I didn't even think of that. "One week," he tells me, "just one more week."

"Dad, I swear to God …" I look down, tears coming to my eyes. "If they hurt her …"

"I know, son," he says, and my mother sniffles, so he covers her hand with his. "I know."

I sit and eat, the food sitting like lead in my stomach. I Face-Time her as soon as I get home, and she must see it on my face. "What's the matter?" she asks.

"Is there something you need to tell me?" I ask her. "Something perhaps you should have maybe called me about?" I see her try to hide a smile and then bite her lower lip. "Yeah," I say.

"So," she starts, and I see that she is in bed, "apparently, my in-laws want me out of their house." She rolls her eyes. "Which I'm more than happy to do."

"But?" I say, and she continues.

"I told the kids," she says, "I'm not keeping anything from them when it has to do with them. Daisy cried because she thought that they would keep her room. Lizzie, well, she was pissed and told me to tell them to take the house because she wants to move anyway."

"Sounds like her mother," I say, smiling now.

"Yeah, so we sat down and talked about moving," she says, and I dread she's going to say she's moving farther away, but I don't give a shit because it's not keeping me away from her. "Yeah, and I also took your name off my list for court."

"I heard," I tell her, almost snapping.

"There is no fucking way I'm going to let them paint you as a bad guy. There is no fucking way they get to touch the only pure thing I've ever had in my life," she says. "No fucking way. I'm a good mom. Actually, I'm a great mom, and I have faith the court will see it."

"You're beautiful," I tell her, looking at her. "So fucking beautiful." She looks down and then up again as I stare into her brown eyes, eyes that were dead, eyes that were broken, eyes that somehow have mended, the cracks gone, shining back to life. "I wanted to come to you tonight, but my father said maybe you're being watched."

"I know. He told me that too," she says. "I almost don't care, but it's only one week."

"I'm still coming over tomorrow," I tell her, and she smiles.

"Okay," she says, yawning. "I miss you." We spend the rest of the night talking about her next painting spree.

I set my alarm for four and make my way to her house. I want to see the kids before they leave for school. So I pull up to the house at seven o'clock sharp, carrying a box of doughnuts in one hand and coffee in the other. I ring the doorbell and hear footsteps coming to the door. Samantha opens it just a little bit and then sees me. Her face lights up. "Oh my goodness," she says, reaching out and dragging me inside. Closing the door and grabbing the box of doughnuts and coffee, she places them on the floor and then jumps into my arms. I grab her around her waist. "I missed you," she says softly and then kisses my lips. "The girls are just getting up."

"I brought doughnuts," I tell her, "and coffee."

"Girls," she yells, getting out of my arms, "look who brought doughnuts." The girls walk to the staircase, rubbing sleep out of their eyes.

Daisy waves with one hand. "Hi, Blake, it's early," she informs me.

"It is, sweet girl, but it's time to get up for school anyway," I tell her, and she comes down the stairs holding on to the railing. I pick her up, kissing her cheek, then put her down. Lizzie is next. "Hey, you," I say, bending down kissing her cheek, when she side hugs me and walks to the kitchen. I sit at the table while Samantha gets the girls ready. They both yell goodbye when they walk out. I get up and start putting the dishes in the dishwasher while I wait for Samantha to come back. When I hear the door close, I know she's back.

"I so can get used to this," she says, walking into the kitchen and wrapping her arms around my waist.

"The doughnuts or the coffee?" I joke with her.

"Definitely the doughnuts." She laughs into my back. I turn the water off, grabbing a towel and drying my hands. "I haven't seen you in four days," she says when I turn in her hands, and her arms go around my neck this time. "You know what that means, right?" she asks me with a twinkle in her eye.

"No," I tell her, reaching around her waist to hug her. "What does that mean?" One hand comes up to move the hair off her shoulder to her back.

"You owe me four days of kisses," she says, getting on her tippy toes. "That's a lot of kissing," she says.

"I think I'm up for the job." I bend to kiss her, my tongue sliding against hers while I pick her up. Her legs wrap around my waist, and I carry her upstairs where we spend the day making up for the four days I was without her.

Chapter Twenty-Seven

Samantha

All week, my stomach was in knots; from the minute the social worker spoke to the girls, my head has been all over the place.

Lizzie told me she asked simple questions like who she did her homework with? Did I yell at them? Did I ever hit them? Who dressed her? I'm sure she asked Daisy the same questions, but she didn't remember.

I hug the girls extra hard the morning of the trial. I tried to keep their routine and tried not to let my nerves show, but I didn't take them for granted—every hug lasted longer, every kiss lasted longer.

Placing my coffee cup on my dresser, I go to my closet and pull out my black pencil skirt with the long-sleeved white chiffon shirt, my heart pounding the whole time I get dressed. My stomach turns, flips, and flops, my armpits start sweating. My shirt criss crosses in the front, and my black pumps complete the outfit. I walk downstairs just as the doorbell rings. I open it up and find Blake in a suit. If he looked good in jeans, he pushes the bar in a suit. His blue suit fits him perfectly, and he pairs it with a baby blue shirt, no tie. The top couple of buttons are unbuttoned, and my hand goes to the inside of his shirt, my finger sliding in. "Look at you all dapper," I tell him as he looks me up and down.

"You look like a sex kitten," he says, and I back up.

"Should I change?" I ask him, but his father comes in followed by his mother. "Is this okay?" I ask them about the outfit. His father just nods his head, and his mother smiles at me.

"You look wonderful," she says, and I can see she is nervous also.

"What time is court?" I ask them. Looking at my watch, I see it's almost eight.

"We need to be there by nine thirty," Henry says, and I breathe out and shake my hands.

"It's going to be fine," Blake tells me, grabbing my one hand.

"I hate them," I say, and everyone looks at me. "I hate them for pushing me like this. I hate them for putting this fear in me. I hate them for not supporting them and making the girls go through this. I just fucking hate them," I finally say. "How long do these things last?"

Henry, who is wearing a black suit, white shirt, and black tie, puts his hands in his pockets. "It can be just today, or it can go on for weeks. It really depends on the judge."

"I won't survive if it's longer than a week," I tell them and look down, a tear escaping.

"We get to make our argument first," Henry says. "So you will take the stand today." He looks at me as I nod my head. "They are going to come at you hard," he says. "They will try to paint you in a really bad light." He puts his head down. "And I have no doubt that they will bring up Blake."

"I don't care," I tell them. "I don't care; we did nothing wrong," I say, holding Blake's hand. "Nothing. Blake has the answers to the questions I had, and that is the truth."

"I know," his father says. I offer them something to drink, but they all decline. Everyone's on pins and needles.

"Excuse me," I say, walking upstairs and closing the door. Putting my hands on my knees, I bend over, breathing heavily. "Oh my God, oh my God." The tears run down my face, and I think I'm going to be sick. A knock on the door startles me.

"Baby." I hear Blake whisper softly. "Let me in."

I open the door, and he takes one look at me. "One last fight," he tells me.

"It's the biggest fight of my life," I reply, and he nods his head. "I'm leaving after this," I tell him. "The girls and I decided we are moving."

"What?" he whispers, and I see his face searching mine.

"Yes," I tell him. "They can have the house; they can have everything in the house. I want nothing."

"Where?" he asks me, and I didn't want to tell him like this. The girls wanted to be here when I told him.

"The girls and I were talking, and we really like this little town that we visited. They have great parks, and the zoo is out of this world." I smile when he finally gets it. "Minus the monkey who tries to steal candy." He comes to me, pulling me into his arms. "I don't want to pressure you," I tell him, and I don't continue because his lips are on mine. And just like that, the nerves go away, my stomach settles, my hands stop shaking, and my heart beats normal.

"I want you and the girls to come down this weekend," he tells me, and I just nod my head. "Stay with me."

"Okay," I whisper to him. "We have to go," I say, smoothing down my skirt.

We don't say anything in the car on the way there. We don't say anything when we walk into the courtroom. I don't even turn my head when my in-laws walk in. They hold their heads high as they sit at the table next to us. I don't even make it seem that my heart is beating so fast I think I may pass out. I put my hands on my lap to stop them from shaking. "Here we go," Henry says under his breath.

The bailiff announces the judge, who walks in and nods at him, opening the file on her desk. "Your honor, the case of Schneider vs. Schneider." He turns. "Please be seated."

The judge starts, "In the interest of not doing any more damage to this relationship, I'm going to skip the opening statements."

Mr. Feldman jumps up. "Your honor." And she puts up her hand.

"I think it's safe to say you are going to tell me what a horrible mother the defendant is"—she leans forward—"but I also have to think about the kids," she says, "and the fact that after this, it will be hard for everyone to move on. So, in the interest of the kids, we shall refrain from the bashing of both sides. You can still cross-examine."

I see Henry turn his head and get a nod from Blake. "Mr. Williams, please call your first witness," she says. My neck gets hot, my knees start to shake, and I don't know if I can do this.

Henry stands up. "Your honor, the defense would like to call its first witness." I hear him say from next to me, and I push my chair away from the table when he puts his hand on my arm. "The defense calls Hailey Williams to the stand."

Chapter Twenty-Eight

Blake

Forty-eight hours earlier . . .

I pull up to Hailey's house with my parents. "This is it," I say to them. "What if she hates me?" I look at them.

"Only one way to find out," my father says. Getting out of the car, he helps my mother out of the backseat.

We walk up the steps to the door, ringing the bell. She has no idea we were on our way, none. And you can see it in her eyes when she opens the door and sees us. Her squeals of happiness echo on the small porch. She opens the screen door, jumping into the arms of my father. "I can't believe you guys came and surprised me," she says. When I finally look at her, her happiness is all over her face. She lets go of my father, going to my mother, who holds her face in her hands.

"My girl is glowing," she says with a smile and tears. "So glowing." She looks down at the floor and then up again.

The sound of a truck behind us makes us turn around. I told one person I was coming and that was Jensen; he needs to be here for Hailey.

I watch him step out of his truck and come up the stairs, nodding at me. "Mom, Dad," Hailey says, moving between them to Jensen's side, "this is Jensen." She grabs his hand, and he brings their hands to his lips.

"It's a pleasure to meet you," he says, and if he wasn't so perfect for her, I might have rolled my eyes.

"This is such a nice surprise," she says and then looks at us. "What's the matter?" She spots it right away.

"Shall we go inside?" my father says, and Hailey nods. Her hand remains in Jensen's as he whispers in her ear.

My mother looks around and tries to make small talk. "This is lovely."

"Cut the bullshit," Hailey says. "What's the matter?"

"Dear, why don't you sit down," my mother urges, and she walks to the couch, sitting on it, with Jensen next to her. My parents sit on the other one, leaving me in front of them. "Blake," my mother says, and I just nod.

"I have something to tell you," I start saying and hold my neck with my hand. "There is no easy way to say this, so I'm just going to say it. I'm in love." Hailey's eyes go wide, and the smile fills her face as tears start to form. "Before you celebrate. I'm in love with Samantha." Just like that, her face drops; my mother and father quickly look at her while Jensen looks like he's going to freak out.

"What?" she whispers and gets up, throwing her hands up. "You have got to be fucking kidding me."

"Honey, hear him out," Jensen says, and she turns and glares at him, but he doesn't stop. "Come and sit down and hear him out, and then if you freak out, you freak out."

She crosses her arms over her chest. "You knew?"

He shakes his head. "I did not, but I think since he dragged your parents here, you should hear him out."

She returns to her seat next to him, and he puts his hand around her shoulder. She leans into him. "Okay. I'm listening."

I take a deep breath. "It started when Crystal and I went to see her before you guys moved here. Then she called me, or I called her, I don't even know anymore," I tell her, and now I start pacing. "She wanted answers; that is how it started."

I look at Hailey and see that the tears are rolling down her face. "She wanted to know how it happened. How you and Eric met."

"What?" she asks on a whisper.

"She wanted to know if he did certain things for you that he didn't do for her. I don't know how it happened, but it just did, and then our conversations got deeper. We spoke every single day. And every single day, she got stronger and stronger, except she refused to leave the house."

"I don't understand," Hailey says.

"Her in-laws started treating her differently when she started to question things. She is actually a ward of the state. She grew up and had no one till she met Eric." I stop talking to see if she is still up to it. "Are you okay?" I ask her.

"I'm fine." She motions with her hand for me to continue.

"Anyway, they took her in and treated her like she was family until she started pointing out that it wasn't your fault that Eric cheated. That it was Eric's fault." I stop, not sure I should repeat the rest. "They told her if she was woman enough or wife enough, he wouldn't have gone elsewhere."

The gasp of shock comes from both Jensen and Hailey, but I don't stop. "It gets better or worse, depending on how you look at it. She found a letter."

Hailey sits up straight. "It was a brown envelope. He left his confession of cheating on her along with the picture of you two on your wedding day."

"Oh my God," she says, putting her hand to her mouth. "Yeah, and if that wasn't enough, he basically told her that she made him, but you completed him."

"Asshole," Jensen says while Hailey just looks down and shakes her head.

"I can't even imagine," she says and looks up. "I don't understand."

"It gets worse," my father finally says. "Her in-laws are suing her for custody of the girls." Jensen gets up now and storms out of the house, slamming the door. "Um," my father says, "perhaps I should make sure he doesn't do anything that will need my assistance."

"Surely, they can't take the kids away from her," Hailey says. "That's crazy."

"They are out for blood," my mother says, getting up and going to her. "They are also kicking her out of the house and tried to seize all her accounts."

"What?" I say, shocked at the last part.

"She didn't want to worry you, but they blocked all her accounts even the one she transferred money into. Luckily, she went every day and took out a little bit at a time because she would be stuck with nothing and two girls to feed."

"I don't understand what this has to do with me?" Hailey asks just when my father walks in the door with a red-faced Jensen who goes to Hailey and kisses her lips.

"I don't know how to ask for this, but she has no one. And Dad doesn't want to put me on the stand. All she has is herself and the letter that Eric …"

"NO!" Jensen says, yelling. "No fucking way is she going in that courtroom."

I don't say anything because I would probably be the same way. "I love her with my whole soul," I start slowly. "I never thought I would be able to love again, but she fixed my broken." I get down in front of Hailey, taking her hands. "And I want to fix her broken. I want the girls to be happy and not live in fear that someone is going to take them away from their mother. I want her to be able to go to the store without feeling shame or fear."

"She has no one." My mother looks at Hailey. "She came and sat in your father's office with the world on her shoulders. She walks with her head down and her shoulders slumped." My mother looks at me. "I noticed when we went to the courthouse. Then she almost shrunk into the floor at the restaurant."

"What do you mean?" Jensen asks.

"She's so afraid of running into her in-laws that she barely leaves the house. She googles paint colors, so she can bring sunshine into her house. She has her fucking groceries delivered by Amazon, for fuck's sake."

"Amazon delivers food?" my mother asks, and my father just shakes his head.

"Hailey, I know you don't have to do this, and I hate myself for even putting you in this place, especially after everything that she put you through."

"She didn't do that," my mother says loud and proud. "She did none of that."

"The only one who can help is you. Eric spoke to you about his family or lack thereof." I get up. "It's the best shot we have."

"You love her," Hailey finally says, getting up and coming to me. "You really, really love her and not because you want to save her, but because she fixed your broken?"

"Yes"—I nod—"with everything I have, I love her. I would carry all her worries on my shoulders. I would step into the ring with the devil for her."

"I don't know if I can do it," she finally says, and I have to accept that. "It's not because of Eric or what I felt for him; it's because I don't want to lose what took me so long to build."

"I understand." I smile at her, my heart broken that I even had to ask her. "It's okay." I grab her and hug her.

"I'm sorry," she cries. "I'm so sorry."

"It's going to be okay. She has Dad on her side," I tell her. "He won't stop fighting and neither will I." I look at her. "I can't apologize for loving her. I won't."

"The heart knows what the heart knows," she finally says. We sit, and she asks us questions about the girls, and Mom fills her in, telling them about their camping trip in the backyard. She stays quiet the whole time, and I look at Jensen, wondering if it's too much for her to take in.

We leave there with her standing on the porch with her arms around Jensen's waist and his arms around her. "It was worth a shot," I say quietly as we make the drive back home.

I get into bed, defeated as I try to think of another way to help when the phone rings, showing me Jensen's name.

"Hello," I say.

"She's in," he says quietly, "but if this breaks her…"

"She has you," I tell him. "She'll be fine."

"She'd better be, or else those fucking people won't know what hit them," he says, hanging up, and I finally release the breath I've been holding.

Chapter Twenty-Nine

Samantha

I don't think I heard right. I thought he said Hailey Williams. Surely, he's mistaken. I look at him in confusion with my mouth open, and he just winks at me while the court door opens, and Hailey walks in. Pure class, I see a man following her, and Nanny right next to him.

They walk to Joanne and Blake and sit next to them, Nanny winking at me and looking over at the Schneiders.

Mr. Feldman jumps up. "Your honor, I object. This witness wasn't on the list."

"I have her on my list," the judge says. "Maybe you didn't get your copy, whatever the case. Please swear in the witness."

I watch Hailey walk up the two steps to the witness stand. "Please raise your right hand," the bailiff starts and proceeds to swear her in.

"Please state your name for the record," Henry tells her.

"Hailey Williams," she says softly while I look at her.

"Ms. Williams, do you know the defendant?" he asks her.

"No," she says, "I do not." She looks at me, and a tear rolls down my cheek. "But we had a mutual person in common."

"Objection, your honor, irrelevant." Mr. Feldman jumps up, and I finally look over at my in-laws. Sitting there glaring at her, they are like vultures waiting to devour their prey.

"I'll be the judge of that," she says. "Proceed."

"Who did you have in common?" Henry asks, knowing full well.

"I was married to her husband," Hailey says, and then she looks at my in-laws with her head held high. "Sorry, that isn't true, the marriage was null and void." She looks at the judge. "I was the secret wife."

"Your honor, this has no relevance to the case," Mr. Feldman says. "Eric Schneider isn't the one on trial here."

"Your honor, this is just to show the court that my client was the main person in the girls' life," he says, and I know it's a loophole.

"Proceed," she tells him. Mr. Feldman sits down, looking down at his papers.

"So how much time would you say Eric spent in your house, pretending to be married to you?" I thought it would hurt a lot more than it did, but it really doesn't.

"He was there for maybe three weeks a month," she says softly and then looks over at me. "Sometimes more."

"When he was at your house, did he call his children?" Henry asks.

"Not that I'm aware of," she answers honestly.

"Did you guys FaceTime them?"

"No"—she shakes her head—"not once."

"Did he, at any time, tell you about his children?"

"No," Hailey says, looking at me, as if she is communicating just with me. "At no time was I aware that Eric was married to someone else or had children."

"When did you find out?" Henry asks, not giving her a chance.

"The day he died," Hailey answers, but she doesn't stop. "The police handed me a brown paper bag with all his things in it."

"How did you find out?" Henry asks her. Hailey leans forward and takes a drink of water from the glass sitting in front of her.

"There were two phones in the bag," she says, a tear leaking out that she wipes away with her thumb. "I thought it was a mistake, so we plugged it in to return it to the rightful owner."

"And then what happened?"

"And then I found out that my life was a lie. I found out he wasn't my husband but someone else's husband. That the family and life he promised me was all a lie. Everything was a lie."

She grabs a tissue now, wiping her eyes.

"That must have been a shock to you," Henry continues, and I almost want to tell him to stop. I look over at the judge who is waiting for her to answer.

"It was, considering he told me he was an orphan."

"Your honor, hearsay," Mr. Feldman objects.

"I'll rephrase," Henry says. "Who was at your wedding?"

"No one," she says. "Just him and me and the judge."

"Your honor, I would like to offer exhibit A." He takes a picture from his stack. "Is this you and Eric?" He shows it to Hailey, who nods her head.

"Yes, that was before my family came in," she says, and Henry hands the picture to the judge.

"Where was Eric's family?" he asks her. Oh, he's good.

"He told me he was an orphan, so he had no family there," she tells him.

"Ms. Williams, would you say that Eric wasn't interested in his children?"

"Objection, your honor."

"I withdraw the question. Ms. Williams, would you say that

Eric was close to his parents?"

"I can't say since he never mentioned them, and when he did, he said they were dead."

"Oh my God." I hear my mother-in-law gasp out.

"No further questions, your honor," he says, and he comes back to sit down next to me. "If he fucks with her, I'm going to eat him alive."

Mr. Feldman looks over at us and sneers. "Ms. Williams, would you consider yourself a scorned woman?"

I see a different side to Hailey. Gone is the soft girl and in its place, she looks like she is ready to fight. She smiles at him and then looks at my in-laws. "Scorned? No. Lied to? Yes."

"So you're here out of revenge?" he asks her.

"No," she says. "I'm here because I figured if Eric didn't even acknowledge his parents, he wouldn't want his kids living with them." Direct hit.

"So you have no reason to be here," he starts and then doesn't give her a chance to answer. "Isn't it true that your brother is dating Ms. Schneider now?"

"I have no idea who my brother is dating."

"Your honor, what does that have to do with anything? My client is allowed to date." Henry stands up.

The judge looks at Mr. Feldman. "I'm watching you, Mr. Feldman."

He puts his hands up. "Ms. Williams, is it true you tried to cash in Eric's life insurance policy?"

"Yes," she answers.

"And is it correct it was denied because of fraud?"

"That would be correct. He used his middle name for all our legal documents, which is why it was approved."

"So it's safe to say that you were angry."

"No, I was too busy trying to piece together my life to be

angry."

"Ms. Williams, were you not angry when the plaintiffs had you served with a cease and desist letter blocking you from attending the funeral?"

"No, but I was sad and broken," she tells him. "I had just lost my husband, or who I thought was my husband, and the plaintiffs blocked me from attending the funeral or talking about him."

"So you didn't attend the funeral?"

"Mr. Feldman, if I did, I would be arrested." She looks at the judge. "There was also a restraining order filed against me."

"By the Plantiffs?"

"I don't know who sent it to me. I didn't bother to sit around memorizing it," she snaps back. "Mr. Feldman, I married a man who was already married. I had no idea, so when he died, and I was blocked from attending the funeral and saying goodbye to him, I wasn't angry; I was sad. I was sad that my husband lied to me; I was sad that our life was a lie, but I was most sad that I didn't get a chance to say goodbye. I wasn't given that chance because the parents who he told me were dead were very much alive."

She shakes her head. "But I get it now why he lied about them. He wasn't vindictive; he wouldn't want this." She raises her hands. "The Eric I knew wouldn't want to drag their kids away from their mother. The Eric who lived with me and married me would not want this dragged out because we are moving on," she says. "The only one vindictive in all this and seeking revenge in all this is Mr. and Mrs. Schneider."

"No further questions, your honor," Mr. Feldman says.

"The court is in recess. We will reconvene in one hour," she says, banging the gavel and stepping off the bench as we all stand.

Hailey walks by us, and the man holds his hands out for her. She goes in them and kisses his lips. "You did amazing," he tells her as she looks back at me. I'm about to say something to her when my in-laws walk past them.

"Adrian?" Nanny says as we all look at her and then back at him as his face goes white. "What are you doing here? Where is Lucille?" she asks him, and his mouth opens and closes.

"Who is Lucille?" Judy asks him, and Nanny finally answers.

"His wife!" she says. "They just moved into the condo next to me."

And the madness breaks out.

Chapter Thirty

Blake

"His wife?" I stand here, not sure I understand what is going on, so Nanny continues, "They moved into the condo next door."

"Adrian," Judy says, looking at him. "What is she talking about?"

Nanny throws up her hands. "You have got to be kidding me," she says. "Well, I guess like father, like son." She shakes her head. "Adrian and his wife, Lucille, who is a lovely lady …" She turns to look at us, then back to Judy and Adrian, who looks down. Ethan and Elliot stand beside him. "They moved into the condo. They downsized because they are now empty nesters."

"Empty nesters?" Judy asks.

"Yes, their daughter is eighteen," Nanny starts. "Oh, I think she is eighteen; I might be wrong. What is her name again?" She looks at Adrian, and he doesn't answer. "Anyway, she just went off to college; she got accepted into University of Houston. Their son, who is named Evan," she says, "he just got married. They have a beautiful little boy."

"Oh my God," Judy says, looking at Adrian. "This isn't true, right?"

Adrian looks down at the floor, and we don't even see Elliot move or hit his father in the face. "You fucking asshole." I spring into action, grabbing him and holding him back. "You motherfucker," he sneers at him.

Judy cries silently by herself, Ethan holding her now. "I can't …"

Everyone looks at Samantha, who slowly walks to her. "I want to be sad for you and hurt for you," she says, and my mother goes to stand beside her, "but I can't. When he sat at that table and told me that if I took care of my wifely duties, Eric wouldn't have left me …"

Jensen now hisses. "Motherfucker," he sneers.

"When you came into my house and spat your shit in my face, gutting me and making me feel like I did something wrong. Telling me that maybe if I stopped harassing him when he was home and had been more understanding, it wouldn't have led to that, or maybe if I had been there for him and caring to his needs, he wouldn't have gone elsewhere." She uses her finger to wipe away a tear. "I guess I should be a bit more compassionate and feel bad for you, but I don't. I feel nothing for you."

"Samantha," Elliot says to her and walks to her, and my father and I both go on alert. "You can't say that."

"I can't?" She turns to him and laughs. "Why not?"

"She's family," he says.

"NO!" she yells out, "she isn't my family. Family holds each other up; family supports each other. Families don't shit on each other to better themselves; they don't fucking cut each other down at the knees. They don't leave them to cry by themselves in the bathroom." I walk to her now, standing beside her.

"SO what?" he says. "You're going to choose him over us?" He points at me.

"Any fucking day of the week," she says proudly. "I just hope

I'm good enough for him. He deserves the best there is, so hopefully, that is me." I put my hands over her shoulders, pulling her to me. "You guys keep this shit up, and I'll make sure you never see the girls."

"You can't take my babies away from me," Judy finally says.

"Wake up," she tells them. "It already happened. We're moving. Far away from here, where they don't have the fear that someone will take them away from their mother," she says but doesn't stop. "Where they won't have to worry if they will end up homeless."

"Samantha," Judy says, and Ethan and Elliot both stop her.

"Mom, let's go," they both say. "It's enough."

Adrian is now standing by their side. "I can explain," he says, walking behind them.

My father stops Mr. Feldman. "You don't pull this case, I'm going to get a subpoena for Lucille." He doesn't say anything, just nods his head and walks off.

I look down at Samantha. "I think I just got my girls," she says, laughing. I lean down and kiss her lips in public.

"Holy shit." I hear Nanny say. "I need a drink."

Samantha looks over at Hailey and leaves my side. She walks up to my sister. "There are no words that I can say to thank you," she finally says, and the tears stream down her cheeks. "Nothing I can say will make what they did to you okay," she continues, and Jensen kisses Hailey's forehead. "I swear I had no idea, none …"

"I know," Hailey says softly, and I see that Crystal is now running into the courtroom.

"What the fuck did I miss?" she says, huffing while Gabe follows her.

"Woman, you didn't even wait for me to stop the fucking car. Are you out of your mind?" he says with his hands on his hips as she rolls her eyes, and he takes in the scene. "Oh, fuck." He walks to Crystal and holds her shoulders as she looks at him. "Just in case you get ahead of yourself."

She shrugs him off. "Oh, for fuck's sake."

Nanny throws her head back and laughs. "I like him."

"Good. You're the only one," Crystal says as Jensen looks down, chuckling.

No one says another word because the bailiff calls the court back. Samantha nods to Hailey and walks back to the table with my father. My family now all sits on her side, so for a woman who started with just me and my mom, she now has her own cheering section.

"It's come to my attention that the plaintiffs have pulled their petition. So with that, I award the children to their mother," she says, and we cheer. But then she holds up her hands. "Off the record, I have to say, Ms. Schneider, from the reports from the social worker, you are doing a wonderful job. My ruling would have been in your favor anyway," she says. Samantha sobs, and my father takes her in his arms. "Court is adjourned," she says and crashes the gavel.

"Thank you," Samantha says to my father. "Thank you so much."

She turns to look at me. "Can we go get the girls?"

I just nod my head. "Yeah, baby, we can."

"We need to celebrate," Nanny says loudly.

"Everyone is invited over to my house," Samantha says and then looks at Hailey. "It's Eric free, but I understand if you don't feel comfortable."

My sister smiles at her. "That would be lovely." She turns to me and smiles. "I can't wait to meet these girls who captured my brother's heart."

She hands her house keys to my mother as we get in the car

and go get the girls. Both of them appear with a worried look on their faces. "Mommy," Lizzie says, holding Daisy's hand.

"Hey, girls," I tell them. "We thought you might want to come have a celebration lunch with us."

"Okay," Daisy says, "is there ice cream?"

"That can be arranged," I tell them as we walk to the car.

"So we went to court today," Samantha starts, and Lizzie stops walking.

"Do we have to go live with Grandma and Grandpa?" she asks while her lower lip trembles.

"No, baby." Samantha shakes her head, and Lizzie runs to her and wraps her arms around her waist while she sobs. Samantha leans down, kissing her head. "It's okay, baby."

We finally manage to get the girls in the car and back to the house. The girls don't notice all the cars, but I do. When they open the door, they both step back. The room is filled with balloons in different shapes from hearts to stars. There are a whole bunch of zoo animals, and I look down and smile when Nanny comes out, shouting, "Surprise," with her hands in the air.

The kids jump up and down and then run to her. "How are my beautiful girls?" she asks them as I look around. My mother and father come out from the kitchen, followed by Crystal, Gabe, Jensen, and Hailey.

"Oh my God," Samantha says next to me. "This is amazing." She looks at me. "So, so amazing."

"It's only starting," I tell her, bending and kissing her.

Chapter Thirty-One

Samantha

I look around the room at all the balloons. "I think they outdid themselves," I tell Blake, who's holding my hand. I walk in and thank everyone for coming. I make eye contact with Hailey and motion to the back door. I see her nod her head, and I follow her out.

She walks down the stairs, taking in the playground structure that Eric built. "We can go swing on the swings?" I tell her, taking off my heels and walking to the structure. She does the same and follows me. I sit on one swing while she sits on the other.

"I really don't know how to start." I laugh and look down. "I've never met my husband's fake wife before." The nerves set in, and she looks down and laughs also.

"I thought it would hurt more," she says, looking down at her feet in the grass and then up at me. "I thought I would break."

"I know. I think I did break," I tell her. "I mean, after the shock came in, and then I felt the hate."

"I did that too," she says. "I would sit on the beach and think about everything we went through."

"I did that too," I tell her. "I would go through these things and then call Blake to find out if he did them for you."

"I'm sorry," she says, looking at me with the biggest tears in her eyes. "I would have never, ever done anything with him had I known."

"I know," I tell her, swinging slowly. "I'm sorry that they stopped you from coming to the funeral."

"Yeah," she says, "but I think it was for the best. Can you imagine?"

"I had them close the casket because I couldn't stand to look at his face." I look down, and the tears fall. "I stood there the whole time watching the casket, trying to ask him why," I say, sniffling. "People would come up to me and tell me what a great guy he was, and I wanted to laugh in their face and say yeah, you should ask his other wife how great he was."

Hailey laughs. "I haven't even read the letter he left me." She looks over. "I don't know if I want to."

"Well, I can tell you it's probably better than the shit he left me," I tell her. "I mean, after I cried over it and questioned my whole am I good enough."

"It was never you." She smiles at me. "It was him."

"I love your brother," I tell her, "which is weird since I haven't told him yet." I look down at my fingers and then back up again. "I mean, I know the whole Frankie thing, and he told me he would never be able to love again. I know this, but I can't help it. I love him. With all my broken pieces and all his broken pieces, maybe we're whole together." The tears fall down my face.

"I think you're the best thing to happen to him. He is the one who came to me," she says. "He drove seven hours to see me and plead your case." She looks down with her own tears falling. "At first, I told him no."

"I understand," I tell her.

"But then I thought of Jensen and his daughter, Mila, and pictured him losing her, and I couldn't do that to you. I couldn't do it."

"So you and Jensen?" I smile at her, and she nods.

"Hands down the best thing that ever happened to me. I loved Eric, but what I feel for Jensen is more. I can't even explain it to anyone. But you …" She looks at me. "You get it."

"I do."

"I wanted kids with Eric." She smiles. "But I was like whatever. With Jensen, I would die to have his child. To give him that. For there to be a part of me and a part of him." She smiles so big. "It would be worth everything. It would be worth all the hurt I've gone through if I could have that one thing."

I look at the door, seeing Lizzie come out toward us. "Hey there, princess, did you meet Hailey?" I tell her, and she looks at Hailey.

"Do you hate us?" she asks her, and Hailey just looks at her. "I know who you are. I heard Uncle Elliot and Uncle Ethan talk about you."

"Honey," I say to her, and Hailey holds her hand up to me, letting Lizzie finish.

"I know Daddy did the wrong thing. I know he lied to you. But …" She looks down with tears brimming her eyes. "But we didn't do that, and if you hate us, so will Blake."

"Oh, baby," Hailey says, getting up, going to her, and stooping down to see her.

"Mommy likes Blake and so do Daisy and me. And with Blake, Mommy doesn't cry anymore. Like ever, not even in secret." I put my hand to my mouth. "So please don't hate us."

"I could never hate you or Daisy or your mom," she tells her while she cries. "Ever, ever." She rubs her face softly.

"So you won't tell Blake not to like us?" she asks her with her eyes so beautiful and clear.

"Silly girls, Blake doesn't like you," she says, and Lizzie gasps in shock. "He loves you."

"Really?" she asks, looking at me with hope in her eyes, and then leans in to whisper, "We're going to move close to him."

"Are you?" She smiles at her. "He's super lucky then."

"I think we should get inside before Jensen sends out a search party," Hailey says, getting to her feet. Lizzie runs ahead of us. "Whatever shit things Eric did, he did two things right." She turns and looks at me as I look back at her.

"I mean. I did help, but yeah. Let's give him that one," I tell her. "You think he's looking down on us?"

"I fucking hope he is so I can tell him that he didn't break us; he unexpectedly made our broken love stories perfect!"

We walk in hand in hand, opening the door and looking around at everyone. Crystal looks at us, making sure Hailey is okay. She gets the nod from Hailey and only then smiles. "There you are," Blake says, coming to us. "Are you okay?" he asks, looking back and forth between us.

"Yeah," Hailey says, "just bonding." She smiles and then walks to Jensen, hugging him and kissing his neck while she talks to him.

"Can we come over this weekend?" I ask him, looking up at him as he looks down at me.

"The girls have already packed their bags, and they're already in the car." He smiles. "Go get your bag ready."

"Okay," I tell him. On the way to my room, I see Henry sitting in the living room talking to Joanne. I walk to them.

"Hey," I say to them, and they both smile at me. "I can't …" I say with tears and a smile. "I can't thank you enough." I shake my head. "What you guys did for me and for the girls, I can never repay you," I tell them.

Joanne gets up first and comes to me, grabbing my face in her hands. "Honey, you already paid us back tenfold," she says with her own tears. "You gave us back *our* boy," she tells me. "You made his eyes shine again. You made him smile again."

Henry now stands. "So consider us even." He kisses my cheek. "Sweetheart," he says, "he waited a long time for this. No matter how much I hate Eric, in the end, he gave us both gifts. We get you three, and you made my boy come back to me. Frankly, I think we owe you." He smiles, and I hug him, trying not to sob against his chest but failing miserably. "Enough tears," he says. "Go get your bags packed."

"Okay." I shake my head at them, walking up the stairs to my room and packing my bag for the weekend.

I'm tossing clothes into a bag when the phone rings. I pick it up. "Hello," I say into the phone.

"Sam, it's Elliot," he says softly.

I stop packing and sit on my bed. "What's wrong?" I ask.

"Nothing, I was calling to check on you and the girls." I try not to pfft out.

"We're fine," I tell him. "We've been hanging on for a while now. But you wouldn't know that," I tell him.

"I know, I know," he starts. "Instead of doing what was right, I followed what my father said, and it was wrong," he breathes out. "I want to make up for it."

"Okay," I tell him.

"Can I maybe come over for dinner or take them to the park tomorrow?"

"We're leaving," I tell him, "for the weekend. But after that, I'm moving."

"What?" he says shocked.

"I can't stay here; for the past two months, I've been a recluse in the house. I can't stay here."

"What about the girls?" he asks me.

"They want to go also," I tell him, "especially after this whole mess. They are happy to go."

"You don't have to do that. We won't bother you or the girls."

"It's too late for that," I tell him. "The damage is done."

"Can I come over when you get back and see the girls?"

I close my eyes, then tip my head back. "Yes." I give in. "I'll call you when we get back."

"Okay," he says softly and disconnects. I toss the phone on the bed and get up to get my clothes. I don't even bother changing what I'm wearing. I walk down the steps and see that everyone is gone.

"Where is everyone?" I ask them, and Blake comes to me.

"Crystal, Hailey, and the guys went back home." He smiles at me. "My parents went home but made me promise we'd go over for breakfast tomorrow morning."

"That sounds like a plan." I smile at him.

I walk out of the house, locking the door, and not once do I look back. "I'm ready," I tell him when I close the door.

He grabs my hand in his, driving us out of town toward his house. He doesn't even make it a secret that we are sharing a room. He asks the girls to pick which room they want, and the girls squeal when they go in the room. So I follow them. In each room, he has added a television and a desk. Along with pink lamps, some rugs, and coloring books for Daisy, but a journal for Lizzie. "Who did all this?" I look at him.

"I just wanted them to feel at home and have their own space," he says, and if I didn't love him before, I love him now.

I don't say anything to him. I just go to him and wrap my arms around his waist, looking at the girls while they find all the new things to keep them busy.

Dinner is quiet and just the four of us. The stress of the past week has finally caught up to us, and we all fall asleep early.

Chapter Thirty-Two

Blake

"I bought a new tent." It is the first thing my mother says when we walk into the house the next day for breakfast. "And we bought a blow-up bed, so we can sleep in there," she tells the girls, dragging them outside to look in the tent.

We walk hand in hand, following the girls outside where they ooh and ahh over the twelve-person tent with three bedrooms. The tent is shaped like a letter T. Two bedrooms on each side with a zip up door and another bedroom in the middle. Each room can be closed. I peek in and see that she bought them all memory foam blow up mattresses on stilts, and it looks like a hotel room instead of a tent. Each girl has their own bed with pink covers.

"This tent is crazy," Samantha says, stepping inside as the girls choose their bed.

"Mommy, can we sleep here today?" Lizzie asks, and Daisy agrees with her.

She looks over at me, and I just shrug my shoulders. I honestly don't give a shit where they sleep as long as they are with me, near me. "I'm dying to try out this bed," my mother says. "The guy at the store said it was the crème de la crème.”

My father comes outside smiling. “Isn't this the coolest tent you've ever seen?” he asks me, ducking to go inside and lie on the bed in the 'master' bedroom. “Joanne, this bed is amazing,” he says.

My mother drags the girls away from the tent to go inside and eat, where they hurry up so they can go back outside to sit in the tent. “I don't think they are going to leave that tent today,” Samantha says, watching them walk outside, or rather run.

“Good, then my plan worked,” my mother says smiling. “Why don't you two go and have alone time?”

Samantha looks at me. “That sounds amazing,” she says, “but I couldn't burden you with them.”

“Burden us?” my father says. “Did you see that tent? It's a condo.” He puts his elbows on the table. “Plus, she bought a television to put in there, and she has Netflix fired up.” He points at my mother.

“I haven't had a Netflix and chill,” she says, putting up her hands, “well, since ever.”

“Mom, you know that's code for sex, right?” I tell her, and she looks at me shocked while Samantha looks down and laughs.

“It is not.” She looks horrified. “Who made that up?” she asks.

“Probably the guy who wanted to watch television and have sex,” my father points out to her.

“Are you guys sure?” Samantha asks. “What if they get scared or on your nerves?”

“If they want to come home at any time, I will bring them to you in a heartbeat, and if you can't sleep without them, you are more than welcome to come here and sleep in the spare bedroom.”

“Okay,” she whispers. “If it's okay with them, I'm okay leaving them."

My mother cheers like she just won the Super Bowl, getting up and going outside to yell for the girls. "She said yes. She said yes." She runs into the tent and then runs back inside. "Henry, quick, get the television, the kids want to watch *Tangled*. It's about Rapunzel," she says with her hands together in glee. "I'll grab the popcorn." She turns and gets the popcorn ready while Samantha and I go outside to see the kids.

"Are you guys sure you want to stay here?" she asks them, and they both yell yes from their "rooms."

We kiss the girls goodbye and walk out of the backyard holding hands. "So …" I turn her to face me. "What do you want to do?"

She walks to me slowly, putting her hands around my neck and going on her tippy toes. "I want to go home with you, lock the door," she leans in and whispers, "and make out with you."

I moan in agreement, leaning down and kissing her lips. "That sounds like a perfect day." We get in the car and head home.

I walk in the house first, tossing the keys on the entrance table. "There is something I need to do," I tell her and then walk to the bedroom and come back with Frankie's picture of us. Standing in the middle of the living room, Samantha looks at me and then at the picture in my hand. Her face falls a little, but she tries to recover. "I've always slept with this picture next to my bed," I tell her, looking down at the picture in my hands. "It got to the point I couldn't sleep without looking at it, and then slowly, it became better."

"Blake." She looks down and up again. "You don't have to choose." She wrings her hands. "I know that you will always love her."

"I will," I tell her, "forever." I look down at Frankie's smile. "But I found out that my heart is big enough to love more than

Frankie," I tell her, and she gasps. "My broken heart got slowly filled; it filled with a new love." She looks at me, smiling, but the tears are flowing. "It filled with a love that seeped itself deeper than my soul; it's in my bones." I walk to the living room and place the picture on the table beside the couch. "It's time for me to live again," I tell her. "I need to live in the present and not the past." I look at her. "You make me want not only the present but the tomorrows."

I walk to her now, holding her face in my hands while she looks up at me with a smile and her face stained with tears. "I want to carry you to my bed and make love to you," I tell her, kissing the one tear that is running down her face. "I want to cherish every single minute we have." I kiss her other side. "I want to go to bed with you in my arms and wake up with you in the morning." I kiss the side of her lips. "I want to fight with you." I kiss the other side. "I want to make up with you." I kiss the other side of her lips. "I want to make breakfast with you." I kiss her lips softly. "Kiss the girls goodbye with you and then at night hold your hand while we watch television." I kiss her again, her hands gripping my shirt on my sides. "I love you, Samantha." I kiss her, this time my tongue licking her lips, and then her tongue is touching mine. Her hands move from my sides to my hands on her face, then they go to my neck as she pushes herself into me.

"I swore I would never love again," she says when our lips separate. "I know it's cliché to never say never, but I was so sure I would never want another man again. Not after everything I went through." She shrugs her shoulders. "But then something shifted in me, like the whole universe was pushing me in this one direction, and that direction was you." She looks down. "I reread all our text messages we've ever sent. At night if you didn't call me, or in the morning after I put the kids on the bus.

You were my lifeline, and you didn't even know," she whispers, "and then you took the broken in me and mended me." She kisses me now. "My lifeline became my salvation." She kisses me. "And my salvation became love." She leans her forehead against my chest and then looks up again. "You, Blake Williams, are what fairy tales are made of."

I lean down to kiss her, the softness still there, but the need more. I pick her up, and this time, she wraps her legs around my waist. Her hands wrap around my neck as I carry her to my bed. I place her down in front of the bed. My hand goes to her neck, her hand goes to the hem of my t-shirt. Lifting it up, she slowly inches it up, her hands on me, her soft touch giving me goose bumps. I watch her hand pull up my shirt until she pulls it over my head. Her fingers tracing down my chest.

My hands go to her button-down shirt now. One button at a time, her eyes are focused on my fingers till I get to the last one. I push the shirt off her shoulders and take a breath because she's so perfect. I lean down, softly kissing all along her shoulder as her fingers rake through my hair.

I kiss her neck, my tongue now coming out to taste her. She moans and gives me more access to her, soft kisses savoring her till I nip her ear, my hands grasping her hips. Her hand leaves, going to my shoulder, down my arm, till she hits my waist. She moves her hand along my waist to the front, unsnapping the button. My hand holds her neck as I look down at her fingers working my zipper down. My chest rising and falling, my heart beats faster than before. Her hand slides inside the front of my jeans, cupping me. I hiss out at her touch while my hips thrust forward on their own.

My lips find hers as our tongues meet. When our mouths meet, our hands and fingers take in each other. One hand cups her breast while the other unsnaps the button to her jeans, and her tongue gets more aggressive once I pull the zipper down. I don't leave her mouth while my hand turns and slides down her stomach, slowly sliding into her panties. My finger slips down, hitting her wetness, and my finger finds her clit. Her hips buck as she gasps and leaves my lips. "Oh my God," she says as my finger enters her. My hand is constricted by her pants, but I get in there enough to move in and out, slowly. Her hips moving into my hand each time. She doesn't just take me; she helps me.

"I need …" she whispers.

"What?" I ask her, kissing her neck, sucking it in. "What do you need?"

"I need you naked," she says while her hand slips into my boxers, her skin on mine as she wraps her hand around my cock. "I need to feel you on me," she says while she slowly thrusts her hips at my hand, mimicking the moves on me with her hand. "I…" She stops talking, and I feel she's close because I can barely move my finger now. I close my eyes, trying not to come too soon, but it may be a losing battle. "I just want you," she says, her voice tapering off when she comes on my finger, her hands stop moving as she rides out her orgasm on my finger.

I take my hand out of her pants, watching her, and I put my finger in my mouth, her breath hitching. "Later," I tell her, "I'm going to spend my time savoring you." I make the promise, pulling her pants down her legs. She steps out of one leg and then the other. I kiss her hip, looking up at her, seeing her eyes on me. I pull her panties down, and if I thought she was perfect before, I was wrong because she isn't perfect, she is magnificent. Her hands repeat the same things with me, pulling my pants down and then my boxers. My cock springs out, and I feel her leaning down to take my cock in her mouth, but I stop her. "If you put that sweet mouth on me, this is going to be over before we even know it."

She smiles at me, wrapping her hand around my shaft. "Well, then later while you savor me, I'll get my own taste." My hands go to the back of her bra where I unclip it, and the straps fall down the sides of her arms and she lets it fall to the floor. My hands move on their own, cupping her breasts in my hands. Her nipples stiffen in my palm.

Her eyes close as I reach down and take one nipple in my mouth, sucking it deep while I roll the other. "Can we do all this," she pants out, "later?"

I let her nipple go, stepping back to look at her. "Are we getting angsty?"

She walks around me now, going to the bed and climbing on top of it on her knees. "Are you going to join me?" she asks over her shoulder as I take in her perfect ass. I don't think we are going to get any sleep.

I walk to my side table, taking out the condoms I bought last weekend. Her eyes widen at the sight of them. "I haven't been with anyone except Eric," she tells me, "and I got tested after he died." She looks down and then up again. "I don't want anything between us …" She then looks back down. "But I get it."

I toss the condoms on the table and get on the bed on my knees, my hands cupping her face. "I would never take you without one unless you asked me to."

"Then I'm asking you to," she says. I lean down and kiss her, and we slide down. Facing each other, we kiss for what seems like hours but is just minutes. I roll her on her back, her legs opening for me.

"Put me in you," I tell her when my forehead touches hers. She moves between us and grabs me, rubbing me through her slit, wetting me as she positions my cock at her entrance, and I slide in one fucking centimeter at a time, the wetness sucking me in. Our moans come out at the same time as she arches her back. I plant myself all the way inside. Her legs wrap around my hips as her hand rubs my back up and down. Our foreheads are pressed against each other as I make love to her. Slowly, her hips tilt back each time, taking me deeper and deeper, and then I can't stop. I thrust harder and faster. Her eyes close as I feel her pussy getting tighter and tighter, our panting breaths coming faster and faster. Until I feel her come, her pussy so tight I don't think I could come out, and I don't. I plant myself inside her and come with a roar.

Chapter Thirty-Three

Samantha

I'm lying on my stomach, my hands bent and under me when I feel soft kisses on my shoulder. Last night was hands down one of the best nights I've ever had. I moan as I stretch, feeling my body ache. I don't think we slept more than an hour without waking up to feel each other. I woke up once with his mouth between my legs only to be flipped over and taken like that. I obviously had to one-up him, so he once woke up with me sliding down his cock. His hands gripped my hips so tight I might have his finger marks on me. Which makes me smile into the pillow.

"Morning," he whispers from beside me, and I feel his hardness on my back, so I moan and arch my back up a little. His hand cups my breast as he rolls the nipple. He doesn't say anything else; we don't need words as he slides back into me. His mouth on my neck, he fills me over and over again. "Fuck," he says right when we both come together.

"I need a shower," I say once I can get my breathing under control.

"Oh, I can come and wash your back," he says, laughing, and

we walk to the shower together. Ninety minutes later, I sit at the table, my wet hair piled on my head, wearing his huge robe while he stands in the kitchen in his shorts making me breakfast. "You're looking good there, Mr. Williams," I say, hiding my smile behind my cup of coffee. He turns and looks over his shoulder with a smirk.

"I need food to keep up with you." He laughs, and I just roll my eyes as the front door opens.

"Hello? Anyone home?" I hear Joanne as the girls come running into the room.

"Mommy!" They both run to me as I open my arms to them.

"Well, hello there." I kiss them both on the head as I have one arm wrapped around each.

"Sorry," Joanne says, coming into the kitchen. "I tried to stall them as much as I could."

I shake my head and smile at her. She looks exhausted. "That's more than okay. How was last night?"

"It was so much fun," Daisy says. "Henry snores."

We all laugh. "Does he?"

"Yup," Daisy says, grabbing a piece of toast that Blake put down. He leans down, kissing the girls' head.

"Did you guys sleep at all?" he asks the girls who now go sit on one of the chairs.

"They slept fine. I, on the other hand, was so worried," Joanne says. "I just had this fear they would wake up and wander."

"Well, thank you," I tell her, "for everything."

"Where is Dad?" Blake asks her.

"He's taking the tent down," she says. "Would you guys like to come over for dinner?" she asks us, and Blake just looks at me while Lizzie and Daisy both answer. "Yes."

"Only if it isn't too much trouble," I tell her as she just looks at me and smiles.

"Never," she says. "Now I'm going home to bake a pie." She walks out, waving back to us.

"I'm going to lie down in my room," Lizzie says, walking to her room, and I snap up and look at Blake to see if he caught that. He just smirks as he puts some eggs on my plate.

"Eat," he says, bending to kiss me as I smile. "Daisy, you hungry?" He looks over at her, and she shakes her head.

"I'm going to my room too," she says, walking away from the table.

"The kids seemed to be settled," Blake says, sitting next to me. Taking my fork, I grab some eggs and put it on my toast. "I like it."

I chew, looking at him. "Yeah?" I lean over to kiss him, brushing my thumb on his lips before I do. "I love you," I tell him, and he smiles the biggest smile I've ever seen on him, and the smile remains until we load our car to go home.

He kisses the girls goodbye, and they mope to the car. He puts his hand in my hair, cupping my face. "You call me when you get in. I have work, so if I don't answer, text me." He kisses my lips soft, ever so fucking soft.

"I will," I tell him and then get into the car and start driving home. The whole time, my heart is sad that I won't be sleeping in his arms, sad that I won't wake up to his smile, sad that the time just goes so fucking fast. "Did you guys have fun?" I ask them when I lower the volume of the movie they are watching.

"Yeah," Lizzie says. "I don't want to go home."

I look ahead. "But it's our home." No one says anything, so I continue, "What would you guys think about moving?"

"I want to," Daisy says.

"But you have all your friends at school and Grandpa and Grandma."

"I made new friends," she informs me.

"Did you?" I ask her, confused. "When?"

"Nanny took us to the park to play, and we made five friends." She holds up her hand with her fingers separated. She always chooses the number five so she can hold up her fingers.

"Yeah," Lizzie says. "Besides, I don't want to see Grandma and Grandpa or Uncle Elliot."

"Honey," I start, "they love you."

"But they don't love you," she says, looking out the window, and I drop the subject for a later date.

We get home, walking in and seeing the balloons still here but floating halfway. "Okay, girls, unpack your bags and put everything in the wash," I tell them as they walk up the stairs, dragging their bags behind them. I walk into the kitchen to open the shades and then the window to let some fresh air in. I take my phone out and call him, but it goes straight to voicemail. "I'm home," I tell him and then grab ingredients from the fridge to start dinner. I don't want to be here; I hate being here.

We sit for dinner, and the girls are not themselves. Gone are the chatty girls, and in there place is Daisy, who said my cooking was boring, and Lizzie, who pushed the food around her plate. "Can we go back to Blake's next weekend?" she asks, looking up.

"I'm sure we could ask. I think he is off." I know he's off because he refused to pack my bag to go home, saying I was just coming back anyway.

The week drags by, and the girls participate in our FaceTime conversations in the morning and at supper. We set him up on the table, and we tell him all about our day. The only time the girls perk up is on Thursday when they know we are leaving to go to Blake's after school since they have no school on Friday.

As soon as we get there, Blake is sitting on the steps outside waiting for us. The kids are excited, yelling his name. He opens

Daisy's door first and takes her out, hugging her in his strong arms. He puts her down to hug Lizzie next, and they both walk inside to put their bags in "their" room. He doesn't even blink an eye before grabbing my face and kissing me. "I missed you so much," he says.

He kisses me until I run out of breath. "I missed you too," I say as he puts his arm around my shoulder, and we walk inside.

The weekend just cements that this is where we are meant to be, especially after dinner on Friday night when Blake sits at the table and says, "So happy my girls are finally home."

When the kids learn that he works the next weekend, their faces drop, but he tells them they have to come anyway so he can have dinner with them. When the weekend comes to an end, we again make our way home, but this time, it's Lizzie who starts the talk. "If we move to Blake's house, can I bring my bed and desk?"

"Um," I say, looking in the rearview mirror while Daisy tells us that she doesn't want her small bed, she wants Blake's big one. We continue the back and forth for over a month, and each time, the girls bring more and more of their stuff. I don't bring up moving in with Blake until one night he plays hardball.

"Move in with me," he says as he enters me in one thrust, a moan coming out of us. The kids are staying at his parents' house, so we can make as much noise as we want. I raise my hips when he thrusts in again and again. He pushes back on his knees, putting one of my legs on his shoulder and going so deep my eyes roll in the back of my head. "Move in with me," he says, slamming into me harder and harder.

"Please," I beg him. I'm about to come when he pulls out of me, and I groan in frustration.

"Move in with me," he says and bangs into me. He brings me to the edge again only to stop right before I come.

"Blake," I say, grabbing his ass and trying to push him back inside me.

"Move in with me," he says, entering me again. "Wake up with me." He presses in again, lifting my hips to get him into me. "Cook with me." His cock rubs against my G-spot. "Please."

"Okay," I say, looking at him, in his eyes, and he smiles and finally lets me come as he follows me right off that cliff.

The next morning when we pick up the kids, we ask them to sit down at the table. I have no idea how I'm going to start this conversation, and I don't have to because Blake takes the lead. "Girls, how would you like to live here," he asks them, "like all the time?"

He looks at Lizzie and then at Daisy, who claps her hands together with glee. Lizzie just smiles at him as she nods.

We ride back home this time, knowing we'll soon be moving. I call Elliot over the next day.

"Hey," I say when I open the door. "Come in."

"Hey, are the girls here?" he asks, and I call them down. Daisy is excited to see him; Lizzie is standoffish and takes Daisy upstairs after a while. "They look good," he says, sitting on the couch.

"They really are good," I tell him as I sit down on the couch, facing him. "I called you over to let you know that we're moving."

"What?" he says in shock, looking at me.

"This isn't our home anymore," I tell him.

"Is this about Blake?" he asks.

"No"—I shake my head—"this is about us not being comfortable here. Us not being happy here."

"Do you really love him?" He leans forward, putting his arms on his knees.

"With everything that I am." I don't even try to lie.

"Eric knew," he says softly as I look at him. "He knew my father had a double life."

"What?" I ask. "How do you know?"

"Well, after we left court, my father came clean. Lucille was his high school sweetheart. They drifted apart and bumped into each other again by chance. Ethan was just born, and well, he felt like my mother put him on the back burner, so he got his attention somewhere else."

"I can't even," I tell him.

"Well, one day Eric found a picture of him with his other two kids, and he knew they were his because the resemblance couldn't be denied. So the next time he went out of town, he followed him, and that's when he ran into Hailey, and well, you know the rest."

"It doesn't matter anymore," I tell him. "It's time for us to all move on. Your parents own this house, according to the papers my lawyer has, so you can inform them that I'll be moving out in the next two weeks."

"What about the kids? Will you stop us from seeing them?"

"Never," I answer him, "but it is their decision if they want to see you or not. You hurt them. Daisy not so much, but Lizzie …" I shake my head. "You were her uncle, and she thought you were on her side, no matter what."

"I am," he says.

"No"—I put my lips together—"you weren't. When she needed someone to stick up for her, you didn't. Instead of fighting to keep her with me, you didn't even try to stop the shit that was happening,"

"They're my parents," he tells me.

"She is your niece, and you just disappeared. You stopped coming, you stopped calling, it just fucking stopped. She lost her father and you."

He shakes his head. "I'm sorry."

"I forgive you, but the damage is done." I get up. "I won't stop you from seeing her or calling, but I will not force her to do anything she doesn't want to do."

He gets up and nods. "I'll make an effort," he promises, and I just nod and then go up and start packing my boxes.

Epilogue One
Samantha

One Month Later . . .

"Let's go, girls," Blake says, walking out of our bedroom down the hallway while putting on his shirt. I stand in the kitchen with my hip against the counter, watching him. "Morning." He comes to me, kissing my lips. "Stop looking at me like that," he whispers into my ear and kisses my neck.

"Like what?" I ask him, hiding my smile.

"Like you're Sylvester the cat, and I'm the bird." He smiles, turning when he hears the girls coming into the room. "You guys have your lunch boxes?" He grabs his keys. "Lizzie, you have your assignment?"

"Yup," she says, coming to me and giving me a kiss. "You think I can go to Kiera's house after school for a sleepover?"

We've been here for two weeks, and it feels like we've been here forever. Our stuff is mixed with his, so it's our home. The girls made their rooms theirs, with little knickknacks, and of course, Nanny took them to Target where they went overboard. I smile because everyone around them showers my kids with unconditional love. They aren't used as pawns on a chess board; they are just loved for them.

And Blake, to say he is over the moon excited is an understatement. He drives the kids to school every morning when he is home even though they have buses. "It's our time," he says, and the girls love it. I walk to the front door to wave my hand at them as the car pulls out of the driveway, then go back inside to clean up from our breakfast. I look in the living room, the picture of Frankie and Blake sits next to the picture of Eric, me, and the kids. Both of them sitting next to a picture that Nanny took when we moved in. Blake has his arm around my shoulder while he holds Daisy in his arms, and Lizzie stands in the middle of us. The smile on everyone's face making our eyes crinkle.

I turn the music on while I walk to the table, picking up the plates; another thing when Blake is home—breakfast is a free-for-all. He would make the kids homemade waffles if they wanted, and he does it with a smile. When he works, the girls and I go by the station and have dinner with him every single night unless he's on a call.

I mean, it's not all smooth sailing. We fight now or, better yet, we argue. One of the arguments is me paying rent or paying for groceries. Well, that was a big one, ending with me slamming his bedroom door. It also was right before he came into the room and made love to me, telling me how he wanted to take care of me.

So I did what any independent woman did, I gave him the idea that I would let him take care of me, without letting him know it wasn't going to be like that. I think he notices when I buy something for the house, or when he comes back from work and the refrigerator is stocked. He looks over at me but never says anything.

We also do things as a family, mostly after dinner—we take

walks to the park or just around the neighborhood. His hand in mine as my girls walk in front of us. With no weight on my shoulders, I couldn't ask for anything else in the world.

I'm so lost in my train of thought I don't hear the phone ringing. I pick it up, not recognizing the number. "Is this Samantha?" the woman asks on the other line.

"Yes, this is she." I walk to the radio, turning it off so I can hear her.

"My name is Elaine Locke, and I'm calling from Child Protection Services." My heart stops, and my neck gets hot. I hold the counter because I'm sure my knees will give out. "I got your name last week from a Mr. Blake Williams when we were called out for a fire at one of our foster homes." Relief lifts off my shoulders. "He mentioned that you just moved into town and had a background in social work."

I don't know what to say. I'm shocked. "Um, yes, that's right."

"Well, we are always understaffed, and we are looking for a part-time social worker. The hours are very flexible, the pay"— she stops talking and then starts again—"it isn't much."

"I …" I don't know what to say.

"Listen, I would love for you to come in, and we can maybe sit down and talk."

"That would be wonderful," I tell her as I wipe tears from the corner of my eyes. "When would you like to meet?"

"How is next Monday at nine a.m.?" she asks, and I take her address right away. We disconnect as soon as Blake walks into the house.

"What's wrong?" he asks me, stopping in his tracks. His back straightens on alert when he sees that my nose is red, and I have tears in my eyes.

"I just got off the phone with Elaine," I tell him, and he walks to the kitchen.

"Oh, yeah," he says, grabbing a coffee cup and pouring the last of the coffee. "I met her last week and gave her your phone number."

"Well, I have a meeting with her on Monday. For a part-time position."

He leans back on the counter, crossing his feet at his ankles while he looks at me. "Isn't that what you want?"

"Yeah, but I didn't think I would be able to find it," I tell him quietly. "You"—I shake my head—"you give me everything."

"I just gave her your name. *You* have to do the interview," he tells me, putting his cup down. "You're doing it again."

"What?" I smile and shrug my shoulders.

"You're giving me that look again," he says, coming to me.

"I like it," he says to me. "I'll like it even more when my cock is inside you." He grabs me around the waist and carries me to our room, where he fucks me the whole time.

Four days later, I walk out of Elaine's office with a smile I can't wipe off my face. I walk to the car, and after getting in, I finally shout with glee. I call Blake right away. "Hey," I say before he can say anything. "I got the job," I tell him, bouncing in the driver's seat. "I start next Monday."

"They are lucky to have you," he finally says softly. "How about we go down to the beach this weekend to celebrate?"

Hailey and Jensen came down last weekend to introduce Mila to her parents. It started a little awkward, but once we got over that hump, it was a great weekend.

Mila and Daisy were like two peas in a pod, with Lizzie making sure they didn't get in trouble, which was quite often. It didn't help that Henry gave them whatever they wanted.

"Do you think it would be okay?" I ask him.

"I do," he says. "Let me call Hailey and I'll call you back."

Well, to say it was more than okay was an understatement. We ended up leaving Thursday instead of Friday so the girls would have an extra beach day. The ride was longer than I thought, and if I heard one more, "Are we there yet?" I thought I would poke my eyeballs out.

Pulling up to the house, I stare out wide-eyed. This is a perfect getaway. Hailey and Jensen walk out of the house when they see our car, then Jensen turns back and yells for Mila, who comes running out to meet us.

"So glad you guys finally got here. I swear if I heard Mila ask are they here yet one more time," Jensen says.

"I'm so glad you're here," Hailey says, coming down and hugging her brother first and then me. "Let me show you around."

She takes us inside, showing us her beautiful house. The master bedroom faces the water. I watch the waves crash onto the shore, and it's almost as if I was here before. She takes us outside. The girls run ahead of us with Mila as their own personal tour guide. "It's beautiful at night," she says, walking down the stairs that lead to the beach. The girls run to the water, squealing when the wave crashes and almost wets them.

My girls look back and wave at us, and I'm so happy I think I'm going to burst. My hands go around Blake's waist as he looks down at me, kissing me. "Love you," he says, and I just nod.

We have dinner at Jensen's house, which is like a private oasis. I swear the girls run straight outside to Mila's new playhouse that Jensen built her. "I don't think we are going to get the kids to leave here," I lean into Blake and tell him as we sit in the outdoor porch area.

"Yeah," Hailey says, coming to sit on the couch next to Jensen, her feet under her, "I'm not supposed to say anything, but the girls already brought their clothes for a sleepover."

"What?" I ask, looking at Blake. "You did this?"

He puts up his hands. "I did not." He tries to hide his smile. "Daisy asked me, and she used the pout." He tries to plead his case. "And then she said she's never had a sleepover at a friend's house."

I shake my head and roll my eyes. "She has you wrapped around her finger, and she plays you just like a fiddle each time she wants something."

Now, he rolls his eyes. "She does not." He turns to his sister. "She doesn't."

Jensen throws his head back, "When Mila was at Henry's, she convinced him to try green nail polish. You Williams men have a soft spot."

Hailey clears her throat. "Are your toes still painted?" She laughs as he turns to glare at her.

"I was napping." And we all laugh.

The girls end up sleeping over at Jensen's with Hailey, who is giving us her house. Crystal is away for the weekend with Gabe, so it's just the two of us. We walk on the beach back toward Hailey's house, the full moon shining bright. My hand in his as I listen to the waves crash into the shore. "I don't know what it is," I start to tell him. "But it's almost therapeutic listening to the ocean waves."

"I guess that is why Hailey loves it so much," he says quietly.

"I dreamed of this beach," I tell him, looking down. "Before we even got here, before we even started being what we are."

"Did you?" he asks as we arrive at the house, and he turns to walk to it.

"I want to sit on the beach," I tell him, and he sits right down, opening his legs so I can sit in the middle. With my back to him and his legs on the outside of mine, we watch the waves crashing. "I was here, with you," I slowly tell him as his arm hugs me from the back. "And I think Frankie was here also. Almost like she was pushing me to you."

"That would probably be her," he says, kissing the side of my head.

"I love you," I tell him, turning my head to the side to look at him, my hand reaching up to hold his face.

"Do you really?" He looks at me with his green eyes, almost an emerald green in the moonlight. "Do you love me enough to spend the rest of your life with me?" he asks as my eyes go big. "Do you love me enough to grow old with me?" My heart speeds up.

"Blake," I whisper as I watch him get to his feet and take something out of his pocket. He gets on one knee in front of me.

"I never thought this moment would come. After Frankie, I just …" he drifts off. "I just never imagined loving anyone the way I loved her." The tears I try to keep at bay escape. "I was wrong. I was so wrong because not only do I love you with every beat of my heart, but I also know that without you, I wouldn't be able to survive. I watch you when you sleep, I listen to you breathe, my hand on your heart as it beats, and my body sits at ease," he says, smiling at me as my lower lip trembles. "I want to help you with the kids; I want to be your shoulder to cry on. I want to celebrate all the milestones that are to come, and I want it to be with you as my wife."

"Blake." My hands cup his face, and I lean in to kiss him, not caring that I didn't answer him. "I can't believe I was lucky enough to find you, or that I'm lucky enough to have your love. To know that you're my best friend and my lover. I want to wake up to you and go to bed with you. I want to come home from work to you; I want to sit on the porch and hold your hand as we wait for the girls to come home. I want to have your babies, so we can have a piece of each of our love live forever." I kiss his lips. "So yes, I'll marry you. Anytime, any place."

"Fuck, I'm so happy you said that 'cause I would hate to have to drag you to that wedding," he says and I laugh while I kiss him out on that beach where I first dreamed of him. A star twinkles in the sky, celebrating with us.

Epilogue Two
Blake

Three years later . . .

"Shh," I say while I rock my son, Carter, to sleep. He just turned eighteen months, and his teeth are coming in. "Don't wake Mommy," I tell him as he looks up at me with my green eyes.

"She isn't feeling well," I tell him. She has been nauseated for the past couple of weeks, and I immediately thought she was pregnant. It seems that I was right. We found out three days ago we are expecting another baby. I smile as I think about her eyes when the plus sign showed up on the test. "I'm giving you another brother or sister," I tell him.

He loves his mom and dad, more mom than dad, but the love he has for his sisters is something so fierce. No matter where they are, he wants to be there. Lizzie is more understanding than Daisy, who still doesn't understand why he just can't poop in the potty. Or why he goes in her room and touches her things. She asked for a lock for her eighth birthday. I shake my head. "What do you want?" I ask him. "Do you want a brother to even things out or would you like another sister?" I ask him, and he looks at the door, expecting them to be there.

"Izzy?" he says his name for Lizzie. "Dayday?" he says for

Daisy.

"Yeah, buddy, I know, but you have to go to sleep," I tell him as he chews his pacifier. He looks at me, his eyes getting heavier and heavier as I continue rocking him long after he falls asleep.

"You going to come back to bed?" my wife asks from the door. Yeah, something I didn't wait long on to put that ring on it. So in front of our family and friends on a beautiful sunny day, she walked down the aisle with her girls next to her, and I vowed to love them all.

"I'm afraid to put him down," I tell her, and I have to say my kids are my weakness. A tear, a pout, or a sad face, and I'll give you whatever you want.

"Blake," she says, "he's sleeping. Put him down." I get up and place him gently in his crib and walk to my wife.

I get into bed behind her and wrap my hands around her stomach. If I didn't know better, I would think she's further along because she already has the small pouch. She falls asleep right away while I listen to her breathe. "I love you," I whisper to her. "Thank you for making my broken whole," I say, and just like that, I follow her into my dreams.

THE END!

Books by Natasha Madison

Southern Wedding Series
Mine To Kiss
Mine To Have
Mine To Cherish
Mine to Love
Mine To Take
Mine To Promise
Mine to Honor
Mine to Keep

The Only One Series
Only One Kiss
Only One Chance
Only One Night
Only One Touch
Only One Regret
Only One Mistake
Only One Love
Only One Forever

Southern Series
Southern Chance
Southern Comfort
Southern Storm
Southern Sunrise
Southern Heart
Southern Heat
Southern Secrets
Southern Sunshine

This Is
This is Crazy
This Is Wild
This Is Love
This Is Forever

Hollywood Royalty
Hollywood Playboy
Hollywood Princess
Hollywood Prince

Something So Series
Something Series
Something So Right
Something So Perfect
Something So Irresistible
Something So Unscripted
Something So BOX SET

Tempt Series
Tempt The Boss
Tempt The Playboy
Tempt The Ex
Tempt The Hookup

Heaven & Hell Series
Hell And Back
Pieces Of Heaven

Love Series
Perfect Love Story
Unexpected Love Story
Broken Love Story

Faux Pas
Mixed Up Love
Until Brandon

Acknowledgments

When I first started this series it was one book, I bought the cover while order ham at the deli counter. The whole story come to me, and then while writing I fell in love with all of them.

My Husband: Thank you for being by my side through this whole thing.

My Kids: Matteo, Michael, and Erica, Thank you for letting me do this. Thank you for being proud of me, I love you honey bunches and oats!

<u>Crystal</u>: My hooker and bestie. What don't you do for me? Everyone needs someone like you in their corner and I am so blessed than you chose to be in mine. I can't begin to thank you for the support, love and encouragement along the way.

<u>Rachel:</u> You are my blurb bitch. Each time you do it without even reading this book and you rocked it. I'm so happy that I didn't give up when you ignored my many messages.

<u>Leigh:</u> You are hands down one of the most genuine person I've ever met thank you so much for guiding me.

<u>Lori:</u> I don't know what I would do without you in my life. You take over and I don't even have to ask or worry because I know everything will be fine, because you're a rock star, I'm also scared of that whip!

<u>Melissa:</u> My cover girl, I have more covers than stories, but I know you won't let me stop. Thank you for sending me covers while I sleep so I don't yell at you before you go to bed. I love you.

<u>Beta girls:</u> Teressa, Natasha M, Lori, Sandy, Yolanda, Yamina. For three weeks I bombarded your messages with chapters and you ate it up. Thank you for holding my hand, telling me when things sucked and for being by my side.

<u>Madison Maniacs:</u> This little group went from two people to so much more and I can't thank you guys enough. This group is my go to, my safe place. You push me and get excited for me and I can't wait to watch us grow even bigger!

<u>Julie:</u> Thank you for taking my book with all it's mistakes and making it pretty, or as pretty as it can be.

<u>BLOGGERS</u>. THANK YOU FOR TAKING A CHANCE ON ME. You give so much of yourself effortlessly and you are the voice that we can't do this without.

<u>My Girls:</u> Sabrina, Melanie, Marie-Eve, Lydia, Shelly, Stephanie, Marisa. Your support during this whole ride has been amazing. I can honestly say without a doubt that I have the best Squad of life!!!!

And Lastly and most importantly to YOU the reader, Without you none of this would be real. So thank you for reading!

* 9 7 8 1 9 9 0 3 7 6 7 6 4 *